By Rowan and Yew

MELISSA HARRISON

Chicken House

2 Palmer Street, Frome, Somerset BA11 1DS
www.chickenhousebooks.com

KU-821-674

DISCARDED

Also by Melissa Harrison
By Ash, Oak and Thorn

Text © Melissa Harrison 2021
Illustration © Lauren O'Hara 2021

First published in Great Britain in 2021
Chicken House
2 Palmer Street
Frome, Somerset BA11 1DS
United Kingdom
www.chickenhousebooks.com

Chicken House/Scholastic Ireland, 89E Lagan Road, Dublin Industrial Estate,
Glasnevin, Dublin D11 HP5F, Republic of Ireland

Melissa Harrison has asserted her right under the Copyright, Designs
and Patents Act 1988 to be identified as the author of this work.

All rights reserved.
No part of this publication may be reproduced or transmitted or utilized in
any form or by any means, electronic, mechanical, photocopying or
otherwise, without the prior permission of the publisher.

Cover and interior design by Helen Crawford-White
Typeset by Dorchester Typesetting Group Ltd
Printed and bound in Great Britain by CPI Group (UK) Ltd, Croydon CR0 4YY

FSC
www.fsc.org
MIX
Paper from
responsible sources
FSC® C020471

1 3 5 7 9 10 8 6 4 2

British Library Cataloguing in Publication data available.

PB ISBN 978-1-913322-13-7
eISBN 978-1-913696-34-4

It is the great migrating time;
the winter visitors – the wild geese,
swans and duck tribe, the redwings
and fieldfares – are all arriving,
while our summer visitors are
taking their leave . . .

B.B., from *Indian Summer*

Contents

Part II Yew

ROWAN

1

Goodbye to all that

*As the Hidden Folk prepare
to set out for Ash Row,
there's a last-minute change in personnel.*

It was the beginning of September, and although
the days were still sunny the nights had begun to
grow cold. In a little park in the heart of a city, the
hips and haws and rowan berries were ripening,
and the first conkers had begun to drop with a
thump; they lay glossy and irresistible under the
horse chestnut trees, some still half-held in their
spiky green casings, some loose among the grass.

Disguised among the leaf litter under a rhodo-
dendron bush were a pair of little bat-skin tents, and
beside them two of the Hidden Folk, each about as
tall as your hand is long, were sitting cross-legged,
making conker bowls. One, in a frogskin onesie,
had a transparent left hand and foot, and was
carefully cutting a line around a conker using a
borrowed knife with 'STANLEY' engraved on it. The

3

other, who was entirely visible and wore a jaunty hat made from an acorn cup, sat nearby, scooping out the white insides of the conker with what looked like a discarded SIM card. Although it was school home-time, and several teenagers sat on the benches eating chips and talking, nobody saw a thing – because they weren't expecting to.

'Done!' said Moss triumphantly, setting the half conker aside. 'Now all we need to do is polish the insides.'

'We've learnt so much from the Hobs about indoor things this summer, so it's nice to show them our outdoor skills,' mused Sorrel, carefully putting the knife away. 'Just think, they might not even have seen a conker before! How weird is that?'

'Very,' said Moss, getting up and doing some gentle stretches. The scars from the cat bite still hurt sometimes, but it helped to move about. It was scary to think how much worse it could have been, so Moss tried not to – especially as their quest to prevent the disappearance of their kind from the Wild World needed to start soon.

All summer, Moss and dear old Cumulus, who had almost vanished, had lived indoors with their new friends Minaret and Macadam in a secret dwelling deep inside a block of flats. Sorrel and

Burnet, who preferred to sleep outdoors, had set up camp in the little park, but they all saw one another every day.

With help from Chip and Bud the squirrels and advice from Spangle the starling the four of them had slowly become used to Hive life, and had developed what Spangle approvingly called 'nous'. They learnt where to go and where not to go, what times of day were safe, and how to move around without being seen by Mortals. That was easy for old Cumulus, being almost transparent these days, and it was something Burnet was good at too, being an intrepid and outdoorsy type. It helped that most of the Mortals didn't take much notice of the Wild World around them, only of each other, and the shops, and the little black slabs they often held in their hands. (Sorrel, being an inventor, thought the black slabs looked incredibly interesting, and spent a lot of time speculating about what they might be.)

'How are you feeling these days?' asked Sorrel now, as they began to polish the insides of the bowls with soft honeysuckle leaves.

'Oh - nearly mended, though it's taken far longer than I expected. I know everyone's been impatient to get home to Ash Row. I'm sorry I've held you all up.'

'Don't be silly, Moss! The time hasn't been wasted, has it? We've made a good start on finding a new role for our kind in the Wild World. Burnet's planted wildflower seeds in every bare bit of earth we can get to, I've been picking up litter every day, and Cumulus's lectures on "Avoiding Poison: A Guide for the Modern Hive-Dweller" were very well attended – even if it was only by slugs.'

'But it hasn't made any difference yet,' said Moss anxiously. 'The people who are fading are still fading – Cumulus, you, Burnet. Perhaps Pan hasn't yet noticed what we're doing, or perhaps we haven't understood Robin Goodfellow's prophecy properly.'

'You mean, *Ash, oak and thorn were at the world's dawn; rowan and yew will make it anew?*' said Sorrel. 'It's still early days, Moss – when we get to your old home, we'll work it all out properly. And anyway, it's been good for us to get to know the Hive a bit, and learn about different creatures and their habits, don't you think? If you stay all your life in one place, you can end up thinking you know every-thing about *everything*, when really all you know about is you and your friends!'

They worked on for a while in companionable silence. Above them the last swallows and house martins wheeled in the blue autumn sky, eating as

6

many insects as they could to give them energy for their long flight to Africa.

'These last few days it's felt like something's in the air, hasn't it?' said Sorrel, after a while. 'I can't quite put my finger on it. Maybe it's just the conkers, and the colder evenings.'

Like all wild creatures, the Hidden Folk can sense the turning of the seasons, just as ladybirds know when to hibernate, and frogs know when to breed.

'I know what you mean,' said Moss. 'And I don't think we're the only ones. Burnet seemed very quiet last night, when we were trapping crickets.'

'Yes,' said Sorrel thoughtfully. 'I think we're all feeling the same, even Cumulus. Change is in the air. It's time.'

When the conker bowls had been polished to a high gloss inside and out, they looked beautiful. Moss carried them carefully as they set out on the familiar route from the little park to Mac and Min's place. At the block of flats a grating led into a dark passageway beneath the ground-floor stairwell; then they crept through the ducts, gaps and corridors that ran below and around the Mortals' flats, arriving at last at the Hobs' cosy dwelling, which was warmed by a copper water pipe. It felt so lovely and welcoming, and for a moment Moss felt stricken at the idea that they must soon set out again, into the unknown.

'Hello, you two! No Burnet with you this evening?' said Macadam. 'That's a shame. What have you got there?'

Smiling, Moss presented the bowls to Mac and Min, who were delighted.

'How extraordinary. You must tell us how you made them!' said Mac.

'Thank you – we'll treasure them for ever!' said Min. 'Now, are you two hungry? You're just in time for dinner – come and eat.'

The dinner table was the Hobs' pride and joy. A paperback book stood on two empty matchboxes; the cover showed a picture of a red train and a Mortal boy wearing spectacles. There was some lettering, too, which meant nothing to any of them, though they did often wonder about the boy and sometimes made up stories about him after dinner, to pass the time.

Sorrel had had the excellent idea of giving all the Faders a hat to wear so that people would know where their faces were, so above one of the cork stools floated a conical pencil shaving, showing where Cumulus was – a fitting replacement for the hat which had blown off when they were riding on pigeons, high above the Hive. Taking a stool next to Dormer, a Hob who lived in the stockroom of a nearby corner shop, Moss wondered how much time they had left before old Cumulus vanished completely. It was a chilling thought.

Mac and Min brought the food and set it down on the table. There was some cheesy pasta pinched from the flat's kitchen, and some bits of apple and plum for dessert. Burnet had taught the Hobs what grew in each season, and now the couple regularly foraged outdoors. There was a lot of wild food in the Hive if you knew where to look for it, and it was full of all sorts of interesting creatures, too.

Just as they were about to eat, there was a cry of 'Hello-hello!' and Burnet bustled in, bringing the delicious fragrance of a September evening. When summer comes to a close and the equinox approaches, you can smell it on the air. Instead of flowers and grass, beneath the usual traffic smell of the Hive was the subtle, autumnal aroma of mushrooms and fallen leaves. For while spring is all about growth, autumn is about decay – and decay is extremely important, because it makes new soil for next year.

'There you are at last!' cried Min. 'Sit down, sit down. Are you hungry?'

'*Starving,*' said Burnet, immediately tucking in – and they all followed suit. For a while, the only sounds were munching, but it wasn't long before the conversation resumed.

'So I've come up with an Excellent Plan,' said Burnet, through a mouthful of cheesy pasta. This came as no surprise to anyone: while Moss had been recovering from the encounter with the cat, Burnet had been spending a lot of time with Spangle and Vesper the sleek city fox. They'd all known their friend was up to something.

'As you all know, I've been spending a lot of time with Spangle and Vesper,' continued Burnet, unnecessarily. 'And between the three of us, we think we've worked out how we can get from here back to Ash Row – when everyone's quite ready, that is.'

'Are we going by pigeon-power again?' asked Moss, who, despite an initial fear of flying, now looked back on their flight with the birds as the happiest of memories.

'We don't need to,' replied Burnet. 'We're actually a lot closer than you'd think. You see, during the hundreds of cuckoo summers that we lived in the ash tree, the Hive got bigger and bigger, until it crept quite close to us. We didn't realize it, because we didn't leave the garden for all that time. When we *did* leave to look for our cousins, we journeyed with the deer in the opposite direction to the Hive, deep into the countryside. Then, of course, we travelled by pigeon to where we are now – and as it turns out, we could well have flown over our old garden! Honestly, it's true. Spangle's been on a recce and worked it out.'

'So . . . we can just walk there?' asked Sorrel, sounding almost disappointed. 'And you don't need me to invent anything?'

'Not quite,' said Burnet. 'Here's the plan. We're going to walk the first bit, along some kind of huge metal pathway Vesper's told me about – but don't worry, Moss, she's going to come with us, to show us the way and keep us safe from cats. The next stage we can do by water. There's a river that passes very close to Ash Row, and flows on to the sea. Sorrel, start thinking about how we can sail on it. Because that'll get us almost all the way home!'

Everyone started talking excitedly, except Cumulus and Dormer, who looked thoughtful. At last, Dormer spoke up.

'I was wondering . . . it's just that I'd miss Moss

so much, and . . . well, would it perhaps be all right if I came too?'

'I don't think that's—' began Burnet, but just then Cumulus's voice came from under the pencil-shaving hat.

'I think that's an *excellent* idea, Dormer. As a Hob, you know a lot about Mortals and Mortal-made things. You'll be invaluable on the journey, especially as' – and here their old friend could be heard to swallow hard – 'especially as I won't be going with you.'

Moss's eyes filled with tears, and Sorrel gasped.

'These last few weeks it's felt as though I'm somehow . . . not quite here, I suppose,' continued Cumulus. 'Dear friends, my travelling days are over. You must all go on without me, but you must never, *ever* give up on our quest to find a new role for our people, so we can stay in the Wild World for ever – do you promise? Because the truth is, I'm going to stay here in the Hive, with Mac and Min. For good.'

2
Making tracks

*At the outskirts of the
city Spangle brings news
of danger to come.*

The Hidden Folk's progress out of the Hive
along the railway line was slow, and took place
mainly in the dark. Then the tracks were mostly
deserted and silent, but once a night the sections
called 'points' would suddenly move, going
'PSSSSSHHHHT-THUNK', making the little
procession jump out of their skins as they tramped
along. The Mortals who looked after the railway
were testing the points to make sure they worked
properly and could help the huge trains change
direction, so for a few minutes it would all
be 'PSSSSSHHHHT-THUNK, PSSSSSHHHHT-
THUNK, PSSSSSHHHHT-THUNK' – and then
the moonlit tracks would be silent and motionless
again. The first time a train thundered past right
next to them, Moss had panicked and had a little

cry, which everyone had been very nice about. Vesper had simply gazed at the Hidden Folk calmly, her beautiful amber eyes willing them to have courage as the huge metal wagons of the freight train roared endlessly by.

Now, dawn was breaking, and they were huddled with Vesper at the very end of a station platform, where it gave way to a tangled embankment and brickwork bright with beautiful graffiti. In a few hours the station would be busy with adult Mortals going to work and Mortal children going to school, but the first passenger services of the day hadn't started yet, so the trains that passed through carried letters and parcels, food destined for supermarkets, or pile after pile of the pale stones known as railway ballast, held in rusty open hoppers.

In the seven nights since the five of them had set out from the heart of the Hive, they'd covered good ground. Sometimes Vesper gave one or two of the Hidden Folk a lift on her back, but it wasn't easy for her, so for most of the time the four little figures trudged along on foot. And every evening it got dark a little sooner, and the night lasted a little longer before the sun rose.

The stations were the best bits. The lights were left on overnight and they were busy with grey mice, who beetled around at top speed looking for scraps the moment the Mortals were gone. Moss tried to flag one down while Vesper was scoffing half a discarded Whopper, but the little creature was far too highly strung to have a sensible conversation with.

A moment later, Dormer, who had fallen behind, came running up to join the others, triumphantly brandishing a white plastic tube with a bend in it. But when Moss asked what it was for, the Hob just smiled and wouldn't say.

On they walked along the stony embankment as the lights of the station faded behind them, threading their way past crisp packets and plastic bottles, discarded spray cans and rotting trainers, sandbags and takeaway cartons and empty plastic bags.

As the birds had finished breeding, they didn't need to sing to show where their territories were – which meant no more dawn choruses to signal the start of each new day. As the sky over the train tracks began to lighten that morning, Moss stood and listened to a single robin in one of the lineside sycamores sing a few melancholy notes before falling quiet.

When the first of the new day's passenger trains rumbled past, the Hidden Folk and Vesper settled down behind an old brick signal box surrounded by a dense thicket of spiny horsetails, a prehistoric-looking plant unchanged since the Old Time. The four tiny figures took off their backpacks and snuggled into the warm white fur of the vixen's belly, and she brought her brush around to shield them from the breeze. In later centuries, Moss would always remember it as the warmest and safest place they had ever slept.

'I really miss Cumulus,' murmured Burnet. 'I know I keep saying it, but I do.'

'Me too,' said Moss, sadly.

'And me,' said Sorrel. 'I know you were house-mates for hundreds of cuckoo summers, but the four of us went through such a lot together, didn't we? It feels so strange not to have our dear friend with us now.'

Moss reached out and gave Dormer's hand a squeeze. It's hard to be the new one in a group, and though Moss tried to make sure Dormer didn't feel left out, it was impossible not to from time to time.

'Min and Mac are the kindest of hosts,' said Dormer, reassuringly. 'I can't think of a better place to spend the winter than next to that nice warm pipe. And as soon as we've found a way to stop our kind disappearing, we'll send for Cumulus, so you can all be together again.'

'If . . . if . . .' began Moss, and then stopped, blinking back tears. It was important to put a brave face on things, seeing as Burnet and Sorrel were Faders now, but it was hard not to be frightened. None of them knew how much time was left until their oldest friend disappeared completely. They had to prove to Pan that they were still needed in the Wild World – and fast.

Burnet sighed. 'I just wish we'd had a proper farewell party. It felt odd to slip away without saying goodbye to all the Hive People. I know it was the safest way, but still.'

'Chip and Bud will understand, and so will the pigeons,' said Dormer. 'The thing is, Burnet, the Hive isn't the same as the countryside. Creatures are always coming and going, so you don't always know your neighbours – and even when you do, it's not always for long.'

Burnet didn't reply, so after a moment Dormer continued, 'Well, anyway: Spangle will explain everything to everyone.'

'Yes, where's that bird got to?' asked Sorrel. 'He was supposed to come and join us, and we've been walking for ages now.'

'He'll find us,' said Burnet, pulling Vesper's soft, fluffy brush over them all like a duvet. 'Let's get some rest. I'm exhausted!'

'Me too,' said Moss. Above them the vixen yawned extravagantly, her tongue a curly pink ribbon, then settled her chin neatly on her paws and closed her eyes.

Moss was woken around lunchtime by a strange tootling noise. Vesper had one eye open, and her brush was twitching. Sorrel was sitting up, looking confused. Burnet gave a loud 'harrumph!' and turned over again, trying to get back to sleep.

Blearily, Moss could see that the sound was coming from Dormer, who was sitting cross-legged in the sunshine and blowing into the white tube the Hob had found on the station platform. The bent end had been trimmed off, and a row of holes had been neatly made in its side.

'What the . . .?' said Moss.

'Erm, hello?' said Sorrel.

'Hi!' replied Dormer, with a smile. 'Isn't it great? I haven't made one of these in years. I'm quite pleased with how it's come out.'

'What is it?' asked Sorrel, who was always keen to know how things worked.

'It's a flute!' replied Dormer, looking a little puzzled. 'You know, a flute. Haven't you ever seen a flute before?'

'I don't . . . think so,' said Moss, going over to have a look. 'What's it for?'

'Well, it's for . . . it's for music. It's an instrument.'

'What, you mean you were making that noise on purpose?' asked Sorrel. 'It wasn't a mistake?'

'Now, look,' said Dormer, a little crossly, 'I know my playing's a bit rusty, but there's no need to be rude.'

'Oh, I'm sorry! I didn't think I was,' said Sorrel, taking the white tube from Dormer and peering closely at it. 'Do you realize it's got a load of holes in it? That's a shame – looks like it leaks.'

'Leaks? Leaks? Of course it leaks! That's where the air comes out when you blow into it. Look!' Dormer snatched the flute back and began to play a little tune. 'See?'

'Ah, I understand,' said Sorrel. 'You're blowing air into it and releasing it by moving your fingers over the holes.'

'Yes! Finally! Have you really never seen a flute before?'

'Never. Have you, Moss?'

'Nope.'

'And so . . . why are you doing it?'

'Because – because that's how you play it!'

'Oh, you're playing with it? Like a game?'

'No – *playing* it. I'm making music! It's an instrument, for Pan's sake!'

Moss was feeling increasingly confused.

'That was your . . . music?' said Moss, hesitantly. 'You mean, like the birds make?'

A train full of Mortals rattled past while they all stood looking at one another in the autumn sunshine. Nobody really knew what to say.

'I just can't believe it,' said Dormer later that afternoon. 'It just . . . doesn't make any sense.'

Vesper had slipped away to hunt rats while the four Hidden Folk ate hot dogs made with smoked caterpillar sausages – a strange new taste for Dormer, but an old favourite for the rest. The caterpillars were stripy orange and black, and had been hoping to become cinnabar moths when they grew up. Sorrel had spotted a crowd of them on some yellow ragwort, and had gently picked four off.

'Of course it makes sense,' replied Burnet.

'Hidden Folk don't need to make music! We live outdoors, surrounded by birds – why would we need to make horrible tootling noises ourselves?'

Moss looked up anxiously; Burnet and Dormer were mostly polite to one another, but they didn't seem to get on as easily as the others did. Sometimes it just happens like that between creatures (and Mortals): nobody can be liked by everybody, and there's no point trying to be, because it stops you being yourself. But while Sorrel wisely kept out of it, Moss wanted everyone to be friends all the time – no matter how impossible that is.

'I'm sure Burnet didn't mean to be rude,' said Moss now, soothingly. 'It's just that we're not used to music that isn't bird-made. But we're all very keen to learn – aren't we, Burnet?'

Burnet made one of those 'Huh!' noises people make when they want to show they don't agree but they're not brave enough to say it out loud.

'Well, *I'd* like to,' continued Moss, loyally. 'So if you can teach me to play tunes on that tube thing, I'm keen to learn.'

'I'll stick to listening to the real stuff, thank you – and I'm sure Vesper will feel the same,' said Burnet, huffily. 'So I'd prefer it if you didn't tootle away around us!'

But as they sat there arguing, something big was approaching: something that would leave a mark on the Wild World and Mortalkind alike. Many miles away, warm air rising over South America had met chilly air over the Atlantic Ocean, and a little funnel of wind had been born. At first the funnel was far out to sea and high up, so it didn't bother anyone, but it was growing – and being carried unstoppably towards the Hive by a current of air known to Mortals as the Jet Stream.

3
The big wind

*Autumn gales force the
adventurers to seek shelter.*

As the group trudged along the railway line, nobody noticed the strong breeze that had sprung up – not even Burnet, who usually kept track of the weather, but instead was thinking of ways to persuade Vesper to travel with them all the way to Ash Row. Like Hobs, her kind still had roots (and relatives) out in the countryside, but now she was a Hive creature, and planned to go back soon. Burnet had a soft spot for her, though, and wanted her to stay.

Yellow ash leaves began to whirl around in the darkening sky. The office buildings and terraced houses that had lined most of the route so far were giving way to playing fields and parks and even small woods; they were still in the Hive, but the outer parts of it had a different feeling to the centre.

The stations were smaller and seemed older somehow, there were more trees, and the air smelt different. Moss was enjoying the change, because they were walking into a world that felt familiar; Dormer, though, felt increasingly uneasy, but was determined to hide it. There had been a bit of teasing about being 'Hive-bound' since they'd set out, and not all of it felt kind – especially when it came from Burnet.

'Evening all, what's occurring?' came a familiar voice – and with a fluster of wings Spangle the starling landed right on Vesper's back. Once upon a time the fox would have whirled and snapped, but she had grown to like the cheeky little bird since they'd met during the hunt for Moss, so she merely twitched her triangular ears and shivered her hackles to say, 'Oh, it's *you* again.'

The others all crowded around, united in their excitement to see Spangle, all talking at once and jumping up and down. Spangle stood up on Vesper's back as tall as he could, stretched out his wings and said, 'All right, all right, all right! Give a bird a break!'

'How's Cumulus?' Moss called out, when it was possible to get a word in.

'And Min and Mac?' added Dormer.

'All good,' said the starling, nodding his sleek little head. 'Cumulus has taken up knitting, and Mac and Min are getting good at Acorn Hop – about which, Chip and Bud are very busy burying 'em all over the park to eat in winter. Acorns, I mean, not your pals!' And here the bird burst into a volley of laughter like a tiny machine gun.

'Oh, it's so good to hear they're all well,' said Moss. 'We were getting worried! Well, I was, anyway.'

'Why?' chirped the starling, fluttering down from the long-suffering fox's shoulders to the ground, where he folded his wings tidily behind his back and began walking along next to them.

'We were expecting you sooner, that's all. We've been walking for days and days now, and I wasn't sure if you'd be able to find us, we've travelled such a long way!'

'First off, you're forgetting how clever I am. Second, didn't nobody explain? I've been busy changing my feathers. Can't believe none of you lot have noticed, come to that.'

The iridescent bird of spring and summer now wore more sober plumage: dark, with a chestnut rim to his wing feathers and neat white spots on his chest and head. As he turned around to show them his new look, the four Hidden Folk all tried to pin the right kind of expression on their faces.

'Yeah, yeah, so it's a bit *boring*,' said Spangle. 'I get it. But I go through two sets a year, see, and I only need a flash set in springtime, for the ladies. Wintertime, I go for a more . . . *underground* look, you get me?'

The Hidden Folk nodded seriously, but Vesper laughed, revealing her four impressive canine teeth.

'Anyways,' continued the starling. 'I got some bad news, though I expect Burnet is way ahead of me.'

Burnet seemed taken aback. 'Me?'

'Yeah, *you*. You know what I'm about to say, am I right?'

Burnet was looking distinctly uncomfortable, while Dormer was trying to suppress a smile.

'The weather!' cried the starling, following it up with a fusillade of clicks and whistles and eye-watering avian swear words.

'Oh! Yes! The weather!' said Burnet importantly, looking hurriedly at the sky and then licking one finger and holding it up to feel the direction of the breeze, which was really more of a wind now. 'Absolutely! The weather is . . . the weather is very . . . it's definitely going to . . .'

'*There's gonna be a massive gale!*' Spangle yelled.

The spiral of air that had built up over the sea had got bigger, and moved towards our islands, growing stronger all the time. A few hours ago its winds had reached the western corner of the country, battering the pretty fishing villages, open moorland, towns and cities with gale-force winds and torrential rain. Birds had fled before it, spreading news of its coming throughout the avian kingdom and further, and every wild creature who heard or sensed the news began searching for somewhere safe to wait the weather out.

Early autumn is a dangerous time for storms to hit, because the leaves are still on the trees; they act as a sail and make it easier for the wind to push the trees over. Some of the birds knew this, and sought out safer places like bushes, mounds of brambles, or thick clumps of ivy. Others went to their usual roosts, only to have to flee in panic hours later, when the storm was at its worst.

Moss and Burnet remembered only too well what a big wind had done to the ash tree they used to live in; weakened, it had split open entirely, destroying their much-loved home. Sorrel was also concerned, having heard the story – and having once lived in an old tree, too. But Dormer was finding it hard to understand why the others were so worried. Hobs, of course, live indoors and only ever hear the weather, rather than experiencing it first-hand.

'Right, we're going to have to find somewhere to shelter,' said Burnet, taking charge. 'Spangle, how long would you say we've got?'

'Couple of hours, max,' said the bird.

'We need to get completely away from the trees,' Burnet continued. 'Vesper, Spangle, you can both cover good ground: how about you head out on a recce? Somewhere that'll fit us all. It won't be easy, but it's not impossible. Moss, Sorrel: can you go through our provisions? Work out exactly how much food we've got, and divide it equally between all our backpacks in case – Pan forbid – we become separated.'

'And what shall I do?' asked Dormer.

'Just . . . try not to get in anyone's way,' snapped Burnet. Moss glanced up and saw Dormer's face fall.

The light was growing dim as the fox and the bird set out, the wind ruffling Vesper's russet fur and whirling Spangle away as soon as he had taken off. While Sorrel and Moss made a pile of all their food and began urgently sorting through it, Burnet set about checking their other equipment was all in order: their tents and spider-silk sleeping bags, their three fishing lines, the 'Stanley' knife, some useful bits of metal wire and coils of rope woven from dried grass.

Dormer, seeing a section of rope with a knot in it, picked it up and began to untangle it.

'Don't touch that,' said Burnet irritably, grabbing it back.

'I was only trying to help!'

'Well, *don't*,' Burnet snapped. 'Everything has to be in order, which means I need to know where everything is.'

'Well, perhaps you shouldn't leave your ropes with knots in them in the first place,' said Dormer. 'Doesn't seem very orderly to me.'

'Please, let's not argue,' pleaded Moss. 'There are far more important things to worry about right now than a bit of old rope.'

'Look, Dormer,' hissed Burnet. 'I know exactly what I'm doing, and I don't need help from *anyone*. All right?'

Having failed to notice the coming storm, Burnet was feeling to blame for their current danger. And that can make you prickly and angry, as most people know: you'll do anything you can to avoid admitting that you made a mistake – including lashing out. That's how Burnet was feeling now.

But Dormer wasn't feeling particularly kind either, given Burnet's constant teasing and rude remarks about the music.

'Well, you *say* you don't need anyone's help,' said the Hob, 'but without Spangle we'd have had no chance to prepare for this so-called storm you're all terrified of. So you might want to think again about *that*.'

'Who's chatting my business?' asked the starling, executing a not-very-graceful three-point landing, hampered by a brisk gust of wind. A yellow-lit train hurtled by, packed with Mortals, its roar adding to the sense of urgency and stress. Burnet stamped off up the embankment in a temper, muttering something about 'Hivies' not knowing anything.

'Oh, nothing,' sighed Sorrel. 'Dormer was just saying how glad we all are that you found us when you did.'

'Are you lot arguing?' whistled Spangle. 'Tell Uncle Spangle the truth.'

'We're worried about the weather, that's all,' replied Moss. 'Did you find anywhere safe we could hide?'

'There's a bin store not far off – it's at the edge of one of those big grassy places where the Mortals kick round things around. You could get under the gate and hide under a bin – might be a bit smelly, but it's the best I've got.'

Sorrel looked up from refastening the backpacks and checking their weight: 'I say we do it. Let's set out as soon as Vesper gets back.'

'Yeah, see . . . the thing is,' said the starling, 'I don't think Vesper'll fit through the bars on the gate. She'd need to find something separate.'

The three looked at one another. It was properly dark now, and the first drops of rain had begun to lash down.

'Shame we're not still in her territory,' continued Spangle. 'Foxes always have a few kennels ready to sleep in, underground or under Mortals' sheds. But round here all the dens belong to other foxes, you get me? Won't be safe for her to go nicking someone else's spot.'

'We can't just leave her the first time we run into trouble,' said Moss. 'She's come this far with us – we should all stick together, I say.'

Just then the vixen materialized, her ears set low against the rain. As they all crouched in the lee of the signal box, she told them about a big burrow

31

she'd discovered nearby – an old badger sett, she thought it was, with room for all of them inside. They'd need to pass under a few trees to get there, so it was best if they set off immediately, before the wind got too strong.

'Badgers?' asked Dormer, sounding doubtful. 'Really? Is this wise?'

'Don't worry, the brocks are our friends,' said Sorrel reassuringly. 'They're also very clean creatures – they even change their bedding regularly. It'll almost certainly be fine. And anyway, what choice do we have? We're not safe here.'

The Hidden Folk shouldered their packs as the fox let Spangle know which direction the sett was in. Then she let out three short sharp barks: a signal she'd agreed on with Burnet when they were exploring, back in the Hive.

Moss watched as a little figure trudged miserably out of the darkness and shouldered the last remaining backpack. Burnet didn't look at Dormer, who didn't look at Burnet. Instead, the Hob, who was at last starting to feel worried about the weather, hurried to hold hands with Moss. As the storm's first big gust buffeted the trees and bushes nearby, the brave little convoy set off into the black and howling gale.

4

Going underground

*Tensions rise as the convoy
waits out the storm.*

Vesper led the way, the white tip of her brush glimmering in the rainy darkness and stopping the others getting lost. In the trackside trees above them, Spangle fluttered from twig to twig, peering down at their progress and calling out encouragement. Unlike owls, whose features quickly get waterlogged in wet weather, the sleek little bird could shake off the worst of the rain, and every so often that's what he did.

Soon they were in a little wood. It was the kind with paths through it, and dog bins, and litter; but once it had been part of a much bigger forest that had covered a huge area. None of the Mortals who walked their dogs there now realized it, but the wood was an ancient place. The trees knew it, though - even those that had only grown there recently, like the rowans and silver birches; and as the Hidden Folk entered it, they could feel it too.

The entrance to the sett lay under the root ball of a beech tree which had fallen down in the famous autumn hurricane of 1987. In fact, the sett had several entrances and exits, and was nearly three centuries old; but one enterprising badger had dug out this particular tunnel to make use of the cavity left by the beech's torn-up roots.

Vesper paused at the sett's entrance and looked back at them as Spangle fluttered down to the forest floor and took up the rear. Foxes do sometimes sleep in badger setts, which can be very large, but as a Hive animal she'd never had to do so before. After a moment's hesitation, she turned her muzzle back to the black tunnel in front of her, crouched a little, and slipped inside.

Like a great many wild creatures, Hidden Folk can see well in the dark, and it wasn't long before Moss's eyes adjusted to the darkness of the sett. Only poor Spangle struggled a little, and could be heard stumbling occasionally and swearing frequently, out of the side of his beak.

The tunnel was broad and quite high, and the walls were worn smooth by the passage of many,

many years of badgers' broad bottoms. Lots of little rootlets dangled from the ceiling, showing where plants and trees grew in the soil above. The tunnel rounded a corner and slanted gently downhill, and the further they travelled along it, the warmer it got and the more distant the sounds of the wind in the upper world became. Every so often they would pass the entrance to a side tunnel, some of which brought fresher air in from the surface, or a stronger smell of earth if they came from deeper down.

They arrived in a large underground chamber with two dark passages leading out and away like mouths. Broad, muscular tree roots coiled through the chamber like pillars, and formed part of one wall. Vesper made them wait while she sniffed every inch of it, checking for any sign that it might still be inhabited – but her nose told her that here, at least, the faint smells she found were weeks old.

'Well, this is brilliant!' said Moss, looking around. 'It may be a bit dank and earthy, but really: what a good place to wait out a storm.'

'It's perfect! Well done, Vesper,' said Burnet.

'You all right there, Spangle?' asked Dormer. The little bird was hunched over and looked thoroughly miserable – a far cry from his usual jaunty and confident manner.

'It's unnatural, that's what it is.'

'What is?' asked Dormer.

'A bird, underground. I don't like it. Some say that one or two of my very distant relations in faraway lands go in for burrowing – but not in these parts, and not this starling. It ain't natural, you get me?'

'It's not for long, Spangle,' said Dormer, soothingly. 'Why don't you tuck your head under your wing and go to sleep? It's got to be past your bedtime by now.'

'Didn't know it would feel like this, or I wouldn't've come. I could've done what I always do, found myself a little nook somewhere,' muttered the bird. 'No skin off my beak. And now I'm down here, in a *hole*, with no sky over me or *nothing*. I ask you.'

Moss stroked the poor starling's hunched back.

'Let's shuffle you over to those tree roots, shall we? If you perch on one of those, you can feel the wood under your feet and know that it carries on, up, up, up above us, up the trunk to all the branches, high in the air. Does that help?'

Together they boosted the bird up on one of the twisted tree roots, where his claws tightened automatically into their roosting position.

'Cheers, Bosses,' Spangle murmured. 'It does help, as a matter of fact. N'night.' And just like that, he went to sleep.

Close by, in the dim chamber dug out centuries before, Vesper settled down watchfully, with her chin on her paws.

'Right, then,' said Burnet, hands on hips. 'How shall we pass the night? I'm not at all tired, is anyone else?'

'Not me,' said Sorrel, while Moss and Dormer shook their heads.

'I know, why don't we play Acorn Hop!' said Burnet.

'I don't think there's enough room,' said Sorrel, doubtfully. 'And anyway, Dormer doesn't know how.'

'It can just be the three of us – you don't mind, do you, Dormer. See? Dormer doesn't mind.'

'Now look, Burnet,' said Moss, firmly. 'I don't think that's fair. We should think of something we can *all* play, or not at all. I know, how about telling stories?'

'All right,' said Burnet. 'I'll start. In the far and distant long-ago time, before Mortals ever came to the Wild World, the first of our kind, Robin Good-fellow, made all Hidden Folk the true and ancient guardians of all the land's loveliest places, and there weren't any Hobs *anywhere*, and . . .'

'That's it. I'm going for a walk,' said Dormer angrily, marching off into one of the tunnels that led out of the chamber – tunnels that led who knows where.

'Come back, Dormer! Dormer, don't go!' cried Moss, calling into the echoing blackness. But it was too late.

'What's got into our friend now?' said Burnet, in an innocent voice.

For the first time ever, Moss felt properly and rightfully furious. Sometimes anger can feel a bit frightening, so it comes out as tears instead. But not this time.

'Burnet, you're behaving really badly, and I'm furious with you,' Moss said firmly, turning around from the dark tunnel and glaring at Burnet.

'*Me?* What have I done?'

'You know exactly what you've done! You've been unkind to Dormer again and again since we set out. You know what it is? It's bullying.'

'What? But *I'm* not a bully! I can't help it if we don't get on!' said Burnet.

Nobody likes to think that they are a bully. Bullying is nasty, yet it's something that most people do, at least once in their lives – usually when they're not feeling safe or good about themselves.

'I agree with Moss,' said Sorrel. 'You've been making Dormer feel left out, and you've been doing it on purpose. I think you should apologize.'

'Dormer should apologize too, then!' muttered Burnet, resentfully. 'Stupid old Hob with stupid spiky hair.'

'Stop it!' Moss said. 'Why are you being like this? You know Dormer isn't stupid, and you know there's nothing wrong with different hairstyles, or clothes, or different anything. So what's *really* bothering you?'

'Oh, all right, I get it: Dormer's perfect,' said Burnet, spitefully. 'Must be nice to have such a *perfect best friend.*'

At this, Vesper raised her muzzle and stared levelly at the three of them. The truth was out in the open, and now there was a chance to mend it. Sometimes it can be painful when that happens, but it's always a good thing in the end.

'Ohhhhhh, you're *jealous!*' said Sorrel. 'So that's it. Well, I never. I didn't think of that, being a relative newcomer to the group myself.'

'Oh, Burnet . . .' said Moss gently. All the anger

was gone, now it was clear how much their friend was hurting.

This time, as the three shared a big hug, it was Burnet who began to cry.

5

Not a pie

Someone with unconventional
table manners drops in.

The tunnel was dark, with many junctions and branches, and Burnet bumped along it, calling Dormer's name. The badger sett was a bit of a labyrinth, and even with Burnet's excellent sense of direction there was a real danger of getting lost.

'Psst! Dormer!' Burnet called out, for the umpteenth time. 'It's me, Burnet. I've come to say how sorry I am, and to make sure you're all right!' But there was no reply.

It was more than a little unsettling not to know who else might be down there. In one side chamber, which smelt strongly of fox, there was a clean chicken bone, a golf ball and a shiny crisp packet; back in spring it had been a nursery for three fox cubs, and those were their toys. In another section, Burnet almost blundered into a busy rabbit warren;

they had dug their smaller tunnels into one of the old sett's escape routes.

'Fitch!' squeaked a doe when she glimpsed Burnet approaching, and all the rabbits fled in terror. It was proof that ferocious stoats and weasels were regular visitors to the labyrinth, too.

Just when Burnet was starting to feel really desperate, worried both for Dormer's safety and about remembering the complicated route back, there came the faint sound of music far ahead in the blackness. It was a simple kind compared to birdsong, but very sad and sweet. After a haunting little melody came a voice quietly singing ancient words that fitted the tune:

> *'Ash, oak and thorn*
> *Were at the world's dawn.*
> *Rowan and yew*
> *Will make it anew . . .'*

Burnet followed the music through several twists and turns and, at last, found the Hob sitting patiently on the tunnel's earth floor playing the white flute, which gleamed in the dimness.

'Hello, Dormer,' said Burnet. 'That was a nice tune. Did you make it up?'

'I can't remember where I heard it, to be honest.

I got lost and felt a bit frightened, so I decided I'd better stay in one place in case I made it worse. I knew that if I made some kind of sound, someone would come eventually.'

'Didn't think it would be me, though, did you?' said Burnet, sitting down too.

'Not really.'

'Look, Dormer. I owe you an apology. Me and Cumulus and Moss lived together for so long – and before Cumulus came, it was just me and Moss! And then we went on our trip and met Sorrel and the four of us had all sorts of adventures together. When Cumulus stayed behind and you came, I felt – I felt as though you might be trying to replace our dear old friend, and also – maybe – to replace *me*.'

'Replace *you*? But you're right here! What in the world do you mean?'

'You and Moss are best friends now, and I feel left out. And because I didn't admit it to myself, or to anyone, it made me behave horribly. I'm really, really sorry. Can we be friends?'

'I'd like that,' said Dormer. 'It's all I wanted from the start – though I did find you a bit scary sometimes. But, Burnet, you need to remember that Moss loves you, and love isn't a pie. Giving a slice to someone else doesn't mean there's less for you.'

43

'*Not a pie . . . not a pie.* I think I get it,' Burnet said, and stood up, with a grin. 'All right, let's get back to the others. I want to teach you Acorn Hop, Burnet's rules!'

When at last Burnet and Dormer found their way back to the others, all thought of Acorn Hop was driven from their minds – for just as they entered the main chamber, the ceiling gave way in a sudden shower of earth which made all of them scream.

There, in a pile of loose soil, lay a sleek black creature with a pointy, snuffly nose, hardly any eyes to speak of, and massive front paws with strong nails like spades.

'Sorry, sorry, sorry,' said the mole, getting up and brushing himself down. 'Happens sometimes. Just passing . . . looking for a worm, I was.' And then he froze, pink nose quivering in Vesper's direction as her amber eyes gleamed back in the darkness and her brush twitched.

'It's all right,' said Burnet, stepping rapidly between the fox and the terrified mole. 'She won't harm you. That's Vesper, and she's our friend.'

'M-m-m-Maurice,' said the mole, extending a

trembling pink paw for the four Hidden Folk to shake. His grip was crushing, even though he was trying to be gentle, and Moss ended up waggling one hand and silently mouthing, 'Ow!'

'Nice to meet you, Maurice,' began Dormer, whose face had taken on the peculiar expression of someone who is about to tell a very bad joke. 'About this worm . . . were you really just passing, or did you mean to . . . *drop in?*'

Moss and Dormer dissolved into snorty giggles, Burnet and Sorrel rolled their eyes at one another, while Vesper cast her eyes up as if to say, 'Oh, for Pan's sake.'

'Dropped in!' said Dormer, nudging Burnet in the ribs and pointing upwards. 'He *dropped in!*' And, raising the white flute, the Hob blew a comical, descending note, like a sad trombone. At that, everyone went completely to pieces – even Vesper, who bared her white teeth and wheezed – while Maurice lay flat on the earth floor among the debris he'd brought down with him, kicking and sobbing with laughter like a velvet sausage with feet. Dormer's joke was terrible, but the sound effect, coupled with the Hidden Folk's relief at being reunited, made them all feel mildly hysterical. Laughing together is such a brilliant feeling: it did them all a world of good, and made them into a team again.

'Oh no,' said Moss at last, dabbing away tears. 'Oh dear. Goodness me. Nobody set me off again. I can't bear it.'

'Yes, no. Oh please. Where were we, anyway?' asked Dormer, trying to be serious again and failing.

'Maurice was just saying he was looking for a worm,' said Moss.

'I was!' said the mole, brushing earth from his whiskers with a huge paw like a pink garden fork. 'See, what I do is, I catches the worms, and then I takes the worms to my special Worm Room, what you calls a larder, and I nips off their 'eads.'

'Oh,' said Dormer, turning a bit pale. Some of the realities of the Wild World can come as a shock to Hive-dwellers, though the sensible ones get over it fairly quickly – something Dormer was determined to do.

'That way,' continued the mole, 'the worms can't tell where they're going, so they can't wriggle orf. And then I goes back for 'em later, when I's peckish. Now, if you lot are off on your travels, this mole says you should copy me. Fresh worms in your backpacks, whenever you want 'em! Nowt in the whole Wild World better'n that.'

'It's certainly inventive,' said Sorrel, cautiously.

'Um . . . yes,' said Moss, 'and yet . . . I'm not sure it's exactly our thing.'

'Suit yourselves,' said Maurice, shrugging his powerful shoulders. 'Anyhoo, it's been terrific to meet some gnomes, as – I'll be 'onest – I thought you lot were all gone. Shame not to meet your bird buddy over there, but I can't say as I blame 'im. If you flew me up into the sky, I'd probably pass out! As for the fox, well, I 'ppreciate not being eaten, but 'er kind and my kind don't have a great history. I'll be off now, I reckon, before 'er changes 'er mind!'

Then Maurice began to scoop aside the packed earth of the chamber floor as though it were bath foam; and in just a few seconds, he had disappeared down and away.

Vesper stood up, stretched, and sniffed the air that came wafting down the entrance tunnel. It told her that a new day had broken, and that the worst of the wind had died down.

6

Now you see it . . .

*With Burnet fading away,
Sorrel's ingenuity is
called for – fast.*

All day, as the last gusts of wind quietened around them, the four little figures and their animal companions tramped around the margins of golf courses and through the scrappy woods that bordered school playgrounds and car parks. It was hard going; the ground was thick with wet leaves brought down by the gale, as well as twigs, conkers, acorns, berries, sycamore samaras, old birds' nests and litter that had been blown out of bins and whirled around all night.

Vesper could trot along perfectly easily, and Spangle was enjoying his release from the world underground, but the Hidden Folk had to fight their way through wet, chest-high debris, which really slowed them down. Dormer also had a lot of new things to take in, which made the whole experience extra-tiring.

By the time the daylight began to fade, they were exhausted, and could go no further.

'But it's only another hour's walk to the river-bank!' shouted Spangle, briefly flying upside-down. 'Come on! Rise above it!'

'I'll rise above *you* in a minute,' muttered Sorrel, darkly.

'What's that?' called the bird.

'Nothing, Spangle. No need to get in a flap.'

'Look, I think we should stop here for the night,' said Burnet. 'We're all tired, and getting grumpy, and there's a risk of us making bad decisions if we can't think straight. Tomorrow we'll get up early and find the river, and then Sorrel can start invent-ing us a boat.'

'All right,' said Moss. 'And also, I'm starving. We need to eat properly if we're going to travel at this pace.'

'Can I help cook?' asked Dormer. 'I'd like to learn. Most of our food in the Hive came from Mortals, so we just had to heat it up.'

As Vesper slipped away to hunt for rabbits on a nearby football pitch and Spangle roosted in a thick evergreen hedge, Sorrel and Burnet put up their four tents: the three grey bat-skin ones, soft and well-camouflaged among the fallen leaves, and one made of cling film pinched from a bin in the corner shop where Dormer used to live. It had once been wrapped around a tuna sandwich, and still smelt faintly of fish, despite everyone's best efforts; worse, when Dormer lay down inside it, everyone else could look in and see, and the poor Hob could see them seeing in, too. It kept the rain off, but it was very peculiar.

'It's not the *best* tent, is it?' said Burnet to Dormer, not for the first time – though in a much kinder voice than before. 'Would you like me to make you a better one?'

'That would be amazing,' replied Dormer, who had got the fire going first time and was extremely proud of it. 'Thanks!'

'You know I like a challenge!' said Burnet. 'Sorrel, will you come with me? In the absence of a helpfully dead bat, your inventiveness will come in handy. We need a material that's thin but strong – and either waterproof or something we can treat somehow . . .'

The pair's voices faded away, leaving just Dormer and Moss beside the crackling orange flames of the little campfire. Working together, they made a chestnut and rosehip casserole. Moss showed Dormer how to remove the hairy seeds from inside the rosehips and explained about the interesting wild foods Hidden Folk traditionally love to eat – some of which are mentioned in their ancient tales from long ago.

'It's weird,' said Dormer, stirring the casserole in its tealight cauldron. 'You can recite ballads and legends going back to the Old Time, can't you? But the oldest stories about Hobs are from when we came to the Hive. It's as though our history only started then, and I've never even noticed it before.'

'But Hobs are just a type of Hidden Folk,' said Moss. 'Before you lived in the Hive, we shared the same past. All our ballads and legends belong to your people, too!'

'Well, we know that *now*,' said Dormer. 'But still . . . stories are important, aren't they? I just wish there was a way to add the story of the Hobs to the great chronicles and sagas – to show that we're part of it too, and that we fit in.'

Just then, Burnet and Sorrel came back to the campsite, triumphantly dragging a large puffball mushroom with a tough outer skin, and the subject was dropped. But Moss understood why Dormer wanted to be included in the Hidden Folk's history, and stored the idea away to think about another time.

That night, the coming winter sent its first frost to find them. The sky was clear, and with no clouds to act as a duvet, the air grew colder and colder. In the silent darkness, tiny ice crystals began to form on the edges of the green grass blades and on the dead leaves, making them sparkle like silver, and killing the more delicate weeds and wild flowers stone dead.

Only the four little tents – three of bat-skin, and one made of the smoked skin of a puffball mushroom – had no frost on them, because they were warmed by the bodies and breath of the four sleeping Hidden Folk. By the time they woke up, the frost had almost vanished, but it was a reminder that colder weather was on its way – and that there was no time to lose.

But the frost wasn't the only worrying thing to happen during the night. At first light Moss was roused by a sad, scared voice from one of the tents.

'Is anyone awake? I think . . . I think my arms have gone,' called Burnet, shakily.

Dormer was the first to rush over.

'Oh, Burnet, I'm so sorry,' said the Hob. 'Can I come in? Are you all right?'

And then Vesper arrived to comfort her friend, and Spangle shook out his feathers and flew down from his roost.

'I'm just a . . . just a torso now, aren't I?' said Burnet, floating out at last into the chilly autumn air. Moss swallowed hard. It was so scary to see dear friends fading away, and not to know if they would ever be properly visible again.

'A torso with a head,' said Dormer, who was trying to be supportive. 'Just think, you could be making all sorts of rude signs with your hands now, and we'd never know.'

'Cheer up, Boss,' chirped Spangle. 'It's not so bad. You're still here, and you're still part of the Wild World, just like the rest of us.'

'But for how long?' replied Burnet, in a shaky voice.

'Right,' said Sorrel, taking charge of proceedings for the very first time. 'I was going to spend a few days building us an amazing boat, like the one the Stream People told me your cousins made for going up the Folly Brook. But it looks as though we don't have time. Good inventors should be able to think on their feet, and that's what I'm going to do. So, Moss: you're on breakfast duty. Burnet and Dormer: pack up the tents. Spangle: fly ahead and work out the quickest route to the water. I'm going to invent something super quickly, like, straight away. *Now.*'

But Moss was paralysed by a sudden, terrifying thought. 'Wait. If Burnet's faded more, what does that mean for Cumulus?'

Shocked, everyone stopped what they were doing.

'May Pan protect us,' whispered Burnet, eyes wide. 'There wasn't much left of Cumulus anyway, being the first of us to start disappearing. What if now . . . what if . . .'

'Let's not panic,' said Dormer. 'Why don't we get Spangle to fly back to the Hive and find out? One way or another, we have to know – right?'

'But we need Spangle for the next part of our journey,' said Sorrel. 'Sailing in my invention will be far too dangerous without an aerial navigator, especially after all that rain we've had – the water's likely to be high!'

'I think Dormer's right,' said Burnet. 'We need to know. I think we'll just have to risk the river without Spangle's help.'

'Well?' asked the starling, looking from Burnet to Sorrel and back. 'What's it to be?'

The four Hidden Folk gazed at one another for a long moment. At last Sorrel nodded. 'Go on, Spangle. Come back as fast as you can, and tell us

Cumulus is all right.'

'I'll try, Boss,' said the starling, and took off.

'Vesper,' Sorrel said, 'I'm going to need your help to gather materials. Will you come with me?'

The vixen nodded, and, deep in conversation, off the pair went.

When Vesper came back she was carrying an empty fizzy drinks bottle in her mouth – quite a big one. She was holding it by the neck, where the lid goes on, but even so, it was a bit awkward, and she kept having to stop to reposition it. Sorrel was trotting along beside her, a bit breathless.

'I saw these things all the time when I was picking up litter in the Hive. I know you're going to say it's not a proper boat and I should invent something better, but there isn't time, and anyway this will be safer, and . . .'

Vesper dropped the bottle, and everyone gathered round.

'We just need to punch some airholes,' Sorrel continued, 'which you can do, Burnet, can't you, and as long as the holes are on the top and we stabilize the base so it doesn't roll too much, then—'

'Wait,' said Dormer. 'You want us to get *inside* that thing?'

'Oh yes, absolutely, I made a smaller version for the Folly once, and it was ever so effective, and if you only need to go with the current, which we do, then—'

'But, Sorrel,' said Burnet, 'how will we make it stop so we can get out? Won't we get washed all the way downriver to the sea?'

'Well, not necessarily . . .'

'Not *necessarily*? That doesn't sound very certain!'

'Almost definitely not. According to Spangle, not far from your old home in Ash Row, there's a fallen tree that goes almost all the way across the water, so that should stop us. Then we just need to find a way to haul ourselves out.'

'Oh, well that's decided, then,' said Burnet. 'Vesper, we need you: you *definitely* can't abandon us now.'

7

The bottle boat

*The four take to the
water, and hope
the risk pays off.*

Moss felt horribly sick. The bottle was floating on its side on the river, moving with the current but occasionally swinging around quite suddenly so it felt as though they were going backwards, or even sideways. There was no way of steering or stopping it, and with only clear plastic above them they all felt very exposed – any passing Mortal could look in and see them, and there was nowhere for them to hide. Thankfully, Vesper had managed to screw the red lid on with her teeth, and the row of air holes Burnet had made stayed above them and didn't let any water in. Sorrel had explained that if they filled the lower half of the bottle with damp earth, packed it down hard and sat on it, it would stop the little craft from rolling – and it worked.

'I hate this, I hate it, I hate it,' muttered Dormer miserably, who was sitting hunched over with eyes screwed tightly closed. Despite feeling seasick, Moss edged over and tried to comfort the poor Hob, who had never even seen a river until an hour ago, let alone travelled on one in a home-made craft.

Burnet and Sorrel were both staring out through the bottle's sides, grimly watching for hazards. They didn't think they'd reach the fallen tree for a good long while, but who knows what else they could hit? As Sorrel had predicted, the river was very high and there were all sorts of things in it, from part-submerged shopping trollies to branches and whirling islands of rubbish and foam, and if they snagged on something midstream, Vesper wouldn't be able to come and pull them out. For as they bobbed and whirled, the vixen was racing along on dry land, somewhere unseen, following the course of the river – running far faster and covering more ground than the Hidden Folk could ever have managed on foot.

The river was much wider than the Folly Brook, and the fast-moving current wasn't clear – though its brown colour came from natural silt, rather than pollution. In fact, it was busy with all sorts of River People, from flounders to water snails, crabs to crayfish, while on the riverbed huddled gangs of grumpy freshwater mussels. There were bits of ancient shipwrecks down there too, and a couple of Roman amulets; there were blood-red garnets half-buried in the silt, and broken clay pipes that glimmered whitely like bone. There were even gold coins and rings that had been lost many centuries before by wealthy Mortals, and now were known only to the huge pike called Gnash, who'd haunted the deep water for over twenty cuckoo summers, baring her rows of terrible teeth and waiting to snatch any barbel, perch or bream who swam by – or any small creature unfortunate enough to fall into her realm.

On the riverbanks were grand old houses with big lawns sloping down to the river, and every so often a huge weeping willow trailed its slender twigs down towards the water, letting all its yellowing leaves be carried away. Some of the houses had little rowing boats or even motor boats tied up at the ends of their gardens, but, thankfully, none were out on the water that day.

'Can we keep to the edges, please? I prefer it when we're close to the edge and not all the way out in the middle, where it's deepest,' said Dormer, shakily.

'Me too,' said Moss. 'It's faster in the middle, and it's making me feel sick.'

'I'm sorry, you two,' said Sorrel, turning away from the view through the clear plastic of the bottle to look at the pair, who were huddled together holding hands. 'Thing is, there's just no way of controlling it. With a few more days, I could have built some kind of rudder, at least, but there wasn't time.'

'Does closing your eyes help?' asked Burnet.

'Yes, a bit,' said Dormer, trying it out.

'No, it makes it worse,' said Moss, and decided to keep them firmly open.

Just then the bottle went into a proper spin, and everyone shrieked and tried to brace themselves against the sides. Water sploshed over the top and a little bit came in through the holes, making everyone wet and adding to the general feeling of things getting really quite dangerous. It was like being on a fairground ride – but with no guarantee that you were going to get off safely at the end of it.

'Hold tight!' shouted Sorrel, as the bottle twirled out of the eddy, caught a swift little current and flew on, cap first, down the river, close to the left bank.

'Everyone all right?' called Burnet. Two little

whimpers from the back showed that Moss and Dormer were hanging on.

'Oh, I do wish Spangle was here,' muttered Sorrel. 'This would be so much less scary if we knew he was up there, watching over us, and taking news of our progress to Vesper. If anything happens to us, she won't even know.'

'I agree,' said Burnet. 'But sometimes things aren't perfect, and you just have to get on with it anyway. We're in Pan's hands – that's who *I* want watching over us, not some cheeky bird.'

While they were talking, the bottle had slowed a little. Moss stopped feeling quite so nauseous, and Dormer sat up a little and opened one eye.

'This is better!' said Dormer. 'Can we carry on like this? I could get used to it.'

But a few moments later the bottle caught on some sticks and dead leaves that had built up at the margins of the river, slowly drifted broadside to the current, and came completely to a halt.

'Oh dear,' said Sorrel.

'Ah,' said Burnet.

'I didn't mean like that,' said Dormer.

There was a long silence.

'What do we do now?' asked Moss.

'Give it a moment,' said Burnet. 'Hopefully the

current will pick us up again.'

So they waited, sitting on the damp earth floor of the bottle and looking at one another expectantly.

Nothing happened. Nothing kept on happening. For quite a long time.

'What should we do?' said Sorrel, eventually.

'How should *I* know? It's your boat,' said Burnet.

'It's not a boat, it's a – a single-hulled catamaran,' replied Sorrel. 'And anyway, you're the one who's good at getting us places. Supposedly, anyway.'

'Er – who was it took charge of everything, first thing this morning? I seem to recall you volunteering to be expedition leader. So this is on *you*.'

Moss began to feel anxious, which always happened when people argued. Cumulus would have said, 'You know it's not your fault when other people get cross with each other. And you don't have to fix it, either!' But Cumulus wasn't with them any more.

'Can you please not argue? It's not helping anything, and I don't like it.'

'Moss is right,' said Dormer. 'Anyway, it's completely obvious what we need to do.'

'Is it?' said Burnet and Sorrel at the same time, both turning around in surprise.

'Of course,' said Dormer. 'It's like when my

cousin Girder got stuck half-in and half-out of a laundry basket while trying to steal a sock. We need to *jiggle* ourselves free. Come on!'

Dormer got up and began to push the wall of the bottle on one side. It moved a little, but not much.

'Help me, Moss!'

So Moss got up too and began to push at the clear plastic in time with Dormer. The bottle began to rock and shift.

'That's it! Keep doing it!' shouted Burnet. 'We're moving!'

'Well, you *could* come and help!' panted Moss.

'I've got a better idea!' said Sorrel, 'We need to jump! All of us! Come on, ready . . . steady . . . *go!*'

If you'd been walking by the river at just that moment, and had looked down at the water, you'd have seen a fizzy drinks bottle with a red lid bobbing rhythmically around as four tiny people jumped up and down inside it, shouting as loudly as they could. Thankfully there were no Mortals nearby to see it – nor the moment when the rocking bottle finally broke away from the twigs and floating debris around it, shifting just enough for the current to catch it, tug at it, and pull it back into the river's flow, where it quickly sailed away and out of sight.

Inside the bottle, everyone was cheering and jumping up and down excitedly on the earth floor.

'We did it! We did it!' yelled Dormer.

'No, *you* did it,' said Moss, proudly. 'Well done, Dormer.'

'Yes! That really was terribly clever,' agreed Sorrel. 'Cumulus did say you'd come in handy, and you have.'

'Thank you, Dormer. I'm so glad you came with us,' added Burnet, with a smile.

'Ooh, we're right in the centre of the river now,' said Moss; then, a little uncertainly, 'Look, everyone!'

They gazed out through the bottle's walls. Moss was right: the bottle was surrounded on all sides by rushing brown water, and the bank where they had recently been stuck was completely out of sight.

'Well, at least we'll make good progress,' said Burnet, who was trying to sound positive. 'We're going *ever* so fast.'

'We really are,' said Sorrel. 'And that's good, isn't it? Fast is good?'

'Oh, absolutely,' said Burnet. 'It's just that—'

'Look out!' Moss screamed, as ahead of them a vast fallen tree surged into view. Seconds later the racing bottle was tossed violently against it, fell back, was tossed again, and at last came to rest close to the river's edge.

But it was the wrong side. Hours ago Vesper had raced off, following the course of the river and looking out for a fallen tree so she could haul them safely out. But the bottle, and its occupants, had washed up on the other bank.

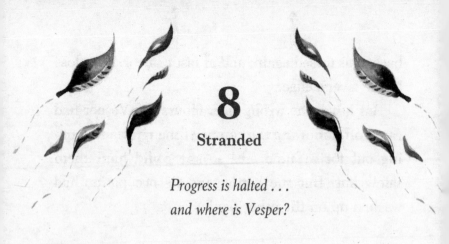

8
Stranded

Progress is halted ...
and where is Vesper?

Nobody would admit it, but it felt to Moss like the most danger they had been in yet. In broad daylight, the four of them were stuck in a plastic bottle, caught against the trunk of a fallen tree and completely visible to any Mortals passing by on the riverbank. From inside, they couldn't twist open the lid to get out of the bottle, and there was absolutely nowhere to hide.

For the Hidden Folk, secrecy is everything. They have lived for many millennia alongside Mortalkind and have been glimpsed so few times that in modern times those sightings have been dismissed as imaginary, or 'just a story' – which is quite an achievement, given that Mortals are so keen on knowing everything about everything, even things which are no concern of theirs. So you can imagine how exposed the four of them now felt, and how frightened they all were.

'All we have to do is wait for Spangle,' said Burnet, over and over. 'When Spangle flies back from the Hive, he'll find us and take a message to Vesper, wherever she's waiting. Then, as long as Vesper can find some way of crossing the river, we'll be all right.'

But they waited all afternoon, the light fading around them, and the starling didn't appear. Twice Mortals walked past on the towpath, talking to one another in their booming voices. Each time it happened, the tiny figures in the bottle floating at the water's edge trembled and shook – but there was nowhere to hide.

'I wish Eddy would swim by,' whispered Moss miserably after a while. 'An otter's what we really need right now.'

'Oh yes, that would be a stroke of luck,' replied Sorrel. 'Like when he fished me out of the Folly back in spring!'

'I suppose we can't always be lucky, that's the problem,' said Moss. 'And I don't think we're going to be this time.'

'What if – what if something happens to Spangle?' hissed Dormer.

'Nothing will happen to him – take my word for it,' Burnet replied.

'Well, *something* happens to starlings. There used to be enormous flocks of them in the Hive, I remember it well! And now there are hardly any. I'm just saying . . .'

'He'll be here. I have a lot of faith in that funny little bird, for some reason,' said Burnet. 'But it could be a bit of a wait. The main thing to do is keep ourselves safe while we wait. Moss, are we all right for food?'

'I think so,' said Moss. 'Shall I check?'

'Good idea. Now, what can we use to disguise ourselves a bit? I don't fancy sitting here waiting for any random Mortal to see us and pick us up.'

'Well, there isn't enough room in here to put up our tents,' said Sorrel, 'but we could just drape them over our heads so that we look like dead leaves, couldn't we? At least until nightfall. Nobody ever spotted our tents in the park, even though there were lots of Mortals about.'

'Good plan.'

'How long have you lived in the Hive, Dormer?' asked Sorrel, as they all began arranging their tent material around them.

'Since before it was a Hive,' replied Dormer. 'But

I can't remember much of that very early time. It feels as though I've always been a Hive-dweller – not like the ones who came in later, from the countryside, and missed it so much. Some of them took a long time to adapt to the indoor life.'

'You were once the guardian of a whole island, weren't you?' said Moss. It felt nice that the others were taking an interest in Dormer. Hearing someone's story – listening to it properly, and asking questions – is a really important way of getting to know them. It's how we come to trust one another, too.

'Oh, it was only tiny,' said Dormer, modestly. 'More of an islet, really. There was a lovely little brook that split in two around it, before carrying on to join the big river downstream. My islet carried on looking much the same, even as Mortals built their funny huts all around it and nearby. Not much changed for me, even when hordes of them came from across the seas and built enormous great stone buildings and amphitheatres and other exciting things; after all, I thought, who can get rid of an islet? I'll be safe enough. But first they built wooden buildings on it, then much bigger ones of brick, and then they sent the whole stream under-ground – can you believe it? No more stream, no more islet. It just got swallowed up by all the streets and buildings, and that's when I moved indoors.'

'Didn't you want to leave the Hive and find another islet, or another stream, out in the country-side?' asked Burnet.

'Not for a second,' Dormer replied. 'I felt like I belonged in the Hive, even though I'd lost the little part of it I loved so much. I still do!'

'So why did you want to come with us?' asked Burnet.

'I suppose . . . I heard all your stories and real-ized the Wild World was a big place and there were lots of different ways to live, and I wanted to see it, not just stay in the same spot with the same people for ever and for ever. And I liked what Cumulus said the first time I met you all, at Mac and Min's party – do you remember? About how good it would feel to help the Wild World. I loved looking after my islet. I want to be useful again.'

The others nodded; all of them felt the same way.

It had got dark while they were talking, which made Moss feel a little safer, though a little way away shone the lights from a riverside restaurant with a terrace that reached out to the water's edge. Although the sun had set, it would not be fully dark until the Mortal day was over and the brightly lit restaurant had closed.

'Well, I think we should eat a little something and then get some shut-eye,' said Burnet. 'What have we got that doesn't need to be cooked on a fire, Moss?'

'Well, I can make us all some acorn bread and sloe jam sandwiches,' said Moss. 'Oh! And how about a dried dragonfly leg each?'

'Not for me, thanks,' said Dormer. 'I'm not saying your food is weird, but dragonfly legs are going to take a bit more getting used to!'

That night, as the four Hidden Folk tried to sleep in the gently bobbing bottle, the first overwintering birds arrived. A flock of redwings, invisible in the night sky above the river, streamed in from chilly Scandinavia, uttering anxious, peeping calls to one another as they flew. Dormer woke up and heard them, and nudged Moss, and the two lay and listened to a sound the indoor-dwelling Hob hadn't heard for nearly two thousand cuckoo summers, and had almost forgotten.

The great autumn migration was underway, when billions of birds move around the globe; over the coming weeks, more redwings, fieldfares and waxwings would arrive to eat the hawthorn berries, sloes and other autumn fruit in hedges, fields and gardens. In would come swans and wild geese – the 'Heaven Hounds' who had once taken one of the Hidden Folk on a great adventure – in great numbers, as well as familiar garden birds like blackbirds who'd been born elsewhere and had delightful accents and different, interesting ideas about life than the ones born here.

For a while now, the summer visitors had been leaving: the house martins and swallows, whitethroats and warblers, the hobbies and harriers and strange-looking nightjars. At last even the persistent little chiffchaffs, the first birds to arrive during the spring migration, were setting off on a perilous journey of several thousand miles. It was a cast change of truly epic proportions, and it always made the Hidden Folk feel anxious and unsettled: they hoped autumn's new arrivals would make it here safely, and worried about whether their departing friends would survive their heroic flight and come back again next spring.

'Hey, do starlings migrate?' whispered Dormer.

'No, they stay here all year,' Moss replied. 'In fact, I think more come from abroad for winter conference season. Why?'

'I was just thinking about Spangle. I hope he comes soon.'

'Me too, Dormer. Me too.'

9

How to be brave

*Spangle brings two kinds
of sad news; but Moss shows
them the way forward.*

At first light, something landed with a thump on the bottle, making it rock wildly and waking everyone up; Moss accidentally let out a scream.

'All alive in there, Bosses?' Spangle said, peering down between his feet.

Four little faces were turned up towards him in fright, peeking out of the folds of tent material. Even seen from underneath, the starling looked bedraggled and exhausted, and for once didn't come out with any of his usual clicks and whistles, jokes or swear words.

'Oh, thank Pan,' said Burnet. 'It's you! I dreamt a Mortal came and picked us up and put us in a bin. When I felt the bottle move, I thought it was coming true.'

'Are you all right, Spangle? You look awful,' said

Sorrel, gathering up the tents.

'Cheers, Boss. You don't look so great yourself,' said Spangle, hopping to the bank and peering in at them through the bottle's side. 'Now, I need to tell you something—'

'How's Cumulus?' interrupted Moss. 'Before we can talk about anything else, we . . . we need to know.'

'Fair enough,' said the starling. 'But you gotta come out of there first. I can't talk to you properly if you're in there and I'm out here.'

'Come out? How do you mean, come out? We can't – that's why we need Vesper,' said Burnet, sounding frustrated. 'And where *is* she, anyway?'

Spangle stared at them all for a moment, open-beaked.

'What? Of course you can get out! You've got a sharp . . . thingy, ain't you? For cutting?'

Everyone turned to stare at Burnet.

Spangle let out a volley of clicks. 'Do you mean to tell me you lot just sat here all night, as helpless as a bunch of voles, when—'

'All right, all right!' shouted Burnet, getting very flustered. 'I forgot, that's all! No need to rub it in, for Pan's sake!'

Nobody wanted to make Burnet feel any worse. As Sorrel tactfully turned away and began to whistle,

75

and Moss and Dormer looked at one another speechlessly, their friend floated on invisible legs to the side of the bottle nearest the fallen tree, took the 'Stanley' knife in an invisible hand and cut a neat hole in the plastic. Then they all stepped quite easily on to the nearest branch, which led them safely up and on to the riverbank.

'Right,' said Burnet, putting the knife away carefully. 'Let us never speak of that again. Now tell us everything.'

'Cumulus has disappeared,' said Spangle, bluntly. 'I'm so sorry to be the one to tell you. I wish it was better news.'

Moss started to cry.

'Gone . . . completely?' whispered Burnet.

'There's a sound from time to time, apparently. I ain't heard it – I don't go into buildings, as you know – but Mac and Min both say they can still hear Cumulus's voice sometimes.'

'Saying what?' asked Sorrel.

'Well, it's . . . it's hard to make out, or so they tell me. Something about a rowan tree?'

'A what?' said Moss, through tears.

The little bird shrugged. 'I don't know, Boss, I'm sorry. I'm so sorry for all of you.'

And they sat down by the riverbank and wept.

'*Psst*,' Spangle said eventually, pecking Dormer gently on the bottom with his beak. The Hob hadn't known Cumulus for as long as the others, and seemed the best one to talk to as they all grieved.

'What is it?' said Dormer, turning around.

'Sorry, Boss. It's just that . . . well, we need to talk about Vesper.'

Dormer stepped away with the starling so they could talk.

'Is she hurt, or something?'

'She's - well, I hate to break it to you, but she's gone.'

'Gone? Gone where?'

'Back to the Hive. She told me she ain't hunted for two days, and she was losing energy. She couldn't get across the water, see? The current's too fast for her to swim it, and the nearest bridge is over a day's fox-trot away, and then it would take as long again to come back along this side.'

'I understand,' said Dormer, 'and I know the others will, too. Just - let me break it to them myself, would you, Spangle?'

'Totally, Boss,' said the starling, sounding

77

relieved. 'But while you're here, shall we have a quick conflab about what happens next?'

'A conflab? Me?' said Dormer. 'Oh no, I think you should talk to one of the others about anything important. I don't know enough about anything to help with making plans.'

The starling cocked his head on one side and fixed Dormer with a beady eye.

'Oh no? Why's that, then?'

'Well, because . . . because I'm nearly the youngest, and I can't even picture this Ash Row place, let alone get us there, and . . .'

'You've got nous, ain't you? And you've got various and assorted bits of knowledge about all things Mortalkind. Way I see it, each one of you is as useful as the others – it's got nothing to do with how many cuckoo summers you've been in the Wild World.'

'Oh!' said Dormer. 'Well, in that case, I suppose . . . why don't you tell me whatever it is, and if I can help, I will. And if not, I'll just have to fetch Sorrel or Burnet.'

'That's the spirit. Now what it is, is this. Ash Row ain't far away now – you're nearly there, in fact – but we gotta cross the centre of town. It's not a big one, but it'll take too long to go all around the edge of it, you get me? So I'm thinking we wait for night-fall and go straight through.'

'That sounds sensible. Is it like the Hive, all brightly lit up with loads of death-chariots?'

'No, much quieter, and not so many Mortals about – especially at night. There are bright lights on big sticks along the busiest part, but there's a quieter way we can go that might be a bit safer.'

'Will we have to cross any death-chariot routes?'

'One or two.'

'I could take charge of that, couldn't I? I've crossed a lot more roads than the others.'

'Smashing idea,' said Spangle, nodding approvingly. 'See? I *told* you you'd be useful.'

Dormer blushed. 'Well, that leaves just one thing to worry about, doesn't it?'

'What's that, then?'

'Cats.'

'Truesay. I always forget you lot can't fly.'

'Who can help protect us, Spangle? We need some kind of bodyguard for this last bit.'

'Big old starling flock, that would be ideal,' said the little bird, looking wistful. 'Like in the olden times. Darkening the sky, wheeling and turning, all diving down together, as one. Oh my days!' Then he shook out his feathers. 'Those times are gone, so back to business. Tell you who'd be handy, if only they'd agree to stay up after nightfall: a couple of magpies. The beaks on 'em are astonishing. And they don't get on with cats, oh no. They got *history*.'

'Good idea – do you know any?'

'Not me, Boss,' said Spangle, shifting uncomfortably from foot to foot.

'Are you . . . scared of them?'

'What, me? Scared? Course not,' said the starling, no longer meeting Dormer's eye. 'I ain't scared of *no* bird. Dunno what you're talking about.'

Dormer started to say something, but then decided to let it go.

'All right. So who's out and about at night and might help four Hidden Folk they've never met before?'

'Well, I know you lot like a wol, but I don't know of any round these ends. There'll be other foxes, but who knows where they're at. Hedgehogs got prickles, but you'll be lucky to find one – they're fading out of the Wild World just like you lot, if you don't mind me saying. So anyways, that leaves bats.'

'*Bats?*'

'I know, Boss. But it's all I got. Most of them'll

be starting to hibernate now, but there's likely a few of them left about.'

'*Bats*, though? Like, *bats*?'

'*Yes*, bats. Look, you and I both know they're the cutest and nicest of all Pan's kingdom, second only to dormice and bumblebees – and yours truly, of course.'

'Oh, of course.'

'But cats don't know that, see? Cats are Mortal-made, they're not wildlife. They don't truly know what us lot are all about. Put yourself in a cat's paws for a second: you've had your stinky dinner-slop, you've done the whole "sweetness and light" act for your Mortals, but you still fancy killing something for a bit of fun. Off you go into the night. You go stalky, stalky, catchy – and then, WHAM! BAM! A load of bats fly all flappy at your head. Scary, right?'

'I mean, I guess?'

'Trust me,' said Spangle, 'I know what I'm doing. Now, you break it to that lot about Vesper, and I'll see you back here at sundown.'

'All right, but . . . where are you going?'

'Well, first I got to eat, you get me? Then I got to have a wash. Then I got to have a kip. And after all that, Pan willing, I'm going to see if I can rustle you up a gang of great big serotines, or maybe even a couple of beefy noctules. All right, your Hobness? Good. Now cheerio.'

The four Hidden Folk spent the day hiding beneath the roots of the fallen tree on the riverbank. They picked at some food, talked, and let themselves feel all their sad feelings about their wise, kind friend, someone who they all – including Dormer – had come to love. The thought of never seeing Cumulus's dear, one-eyed face again was so painful, as was the thought that they hadn't been there to say goodbye. They all had to do some crying, and they all needed to talk about what they would most miss about their friend.

Burnet, Sorrel and Moss took Dormer's news about Vesper surprisingly well; for one thing, they all knew what it was like to be tired and worried and a long way from home.

'I can't blame her,' said Burnet, sadly. 'I really can't. I'll miss her, though. I think I – I love her, a little bit.'

'I feel like we'll see Vesper again, Burnet,' said Moss. 'I don't know why. I just do.'

'I believe we'll see Cumulus again, too,' said Burnet stoutly.

'But – no Fader has *ever* reappeared,' said Sorrel. 'Isn't that right, Dormer? I don't mean to dash your hopes, but looking at the facts, Burnet, when we're gone, we're gone.'

'I'm afraid that's true,' said Dormer. 'Some of our Faders lingered on as voices for a little while, but – oh, I'm so sorry to say it – not for very long.'

'That may be true,' replied Moss, 'but that was before *we* came along. No offence, dearest Dormer, but you Hobs seem just to have accepted your fate. Well, as far as I'm concerned, it's not over until it's over, and if Cumulus can still be heard – even faintly – it's not over yet. Isn't that right, Sorrel? Burnet?'

'I suppose so . . .' said Sorrel, doubtfully, and Burnet managed a tiny nod.

'Look, we can't just give up on our plan to get to Ash Row and find the Mortal child,' said Moss, firmly. 'If we give up, then we definitely know what'll happen: Cumulus will be gone, and our kind will fade from the Wild World, one by one, until there are none of us left. But as long as we keep trying, there's always, *always* hope.'

'But it's hard, hoping,' said Burnet. 'It means you can be disappointed.'

'You know what, Burnet: that's true,' said Sorrel. 'I've felt like that when I've been inventing things and it's gone wrong. Giving up is less effort, and it makes things feel more certain, which is a relief sometimes, isn't it? But one thing I've learnt is that it's just not very . . . it's not very . . .'

Sorrel's face was scrunched up in concentration.

'Not very what?' asked Moss.

'It's not very *brave*,' concluded Sorrel.

Burnet winced. 'But I don't want to think of myself as a coward. I've always thought of myself as a courageous person.'

'You *are*, Burnet,' said Dormer.

'Look, we all want to be brave, don't we?' said Moss. 'Well, this is how we do it: we keep on trying, even if we don't know if it's working, or how things will turn out. That's what courage means.'

10

Crosstown traffic

Can pipistrelles
be bodyguards? We'll
soon find out!

It was a chilly afternoon, and on the riverbank the leaves were drifting down: small yellow ash leaves, familiar to Moss and Burnet from their old home at Ash Row; brown oak leaves with wavy edges, which Sorrel knew well from the Oak Pool by the Folly Brook; big orange leaves with points, which Dormer recognized as being from plane trees, like the tall ones in the Hive.

It took them all afternoon, but the four emptied the earth from the plastic bottle and dragged it to a bin by the riverside path. Burnet then threw up a line of string attached to a wire hook, climbed up, cast the hook and rope down to the others and together they heaved the bottle up into the bin.

At last it began to grow dark, and the constellation that Mortals call Orion and the Hidden Folk call Pan rose slowly behind the rooftops of the nearby town. It was an indication that winter was coming, while to Moss and Burnet it was also a sign of Pan's protection, and they were glad to see its shape there, looking down on them below.

Moss lit a fire by striking two flints into some dry lichen kindling and prepared a quick meal of acorn fritters. Then they all settled down to wait for Spangle – and whoever he might bring.

'Long time since I properly met a bat,' said Burnet.

'Not sure I ever have,' replied Sorrel. 'I used to know one or two Daubentons to wave to when they came to hunt mayflies over the Folly, but we were never properly introduced.'

'I knew a couple of brown long-eared bats once,' said Dormer. 'They used to spend the winter in the attic of a building I lived in, back when Mortal houses were more welcoming. They'd let bats and birds and all sorts of creatures share their homes back then!'

'A long-eared bat would make a good bodyguard, don't you think?' said Burnet. 'Their ears are *very* surprising to look at. I think one of those would give a cat a fright.'

'I don't mind what kind they are, really,' said

Sorrel, 'as long as it's not a couple of those tiny, useless little—'

'All right, Bosses?' said Spangle, landing next to them in the twilight. 'May I introduce Pip and Squeak, currently circling somewhere above us, who, as you can see, are—'

'Not pipistrelles!' said Sorrel and Burnet together, with a groan.

'How rude!' came an impossibly high voice above them, the Wild Argot sounding like the squeak of a wet finger on glass.

'I've half a mind to *flap off*!' came another voice from the dimness, amid the faintest flicker of black wings. 'And to think, we were all set to hibernate tonight!'

'Oh, for Pan's sake,' muttered Spangle. 'I can't believe you lot sometimes. You'd better apologize. *Now.*'

Burnet and Sorrel were nudging each other and hissing crossly, 'You do it!' 'No, *you* do it!' so Moss stepped forward and looked up into the dark sky.

'We're very sorry, Squeak and Pip!'

'We do really need your help,' added Dormer. 'Please ignore our bad-mannered friends.'

Although it was a bit hard to tell because of the

fading, Sorrel was slapping ineffectively at Burnet with both hands, while Burnet, whose limbs were completely invisible, was sneakily trying to tread on Sorrel's one visible foot.

'I dunno, *some people*,' sighed Spangle, before marching up to them, opening his beak and shouting, 'Oi! Give it a rest!'

The two tiny bats, each small enough to fold up and fit in a matchbox, fluttered lower and lower until they were flickering in circles only a few feet over everyone's heads.

'I think they're elves,' squeaked the one called Pip.

'I agree,' piped Squeak. 'They can't *really* be Hidden Folk – those are just made-up. That's what my mammy always told me, anyway.'

'We *are* Hidden Folk,' said Dormer. 'Even me, and I'm a Hob – but let's not get into that. Anyway, thank you for agreeing to escort us across town, and sorry for holding up your plans to hibernate.'

'That's more like it,' said Pip. 'Glad to see at least *some* of you are mature. Now, where did you say you were wanting to go?'

'Ash Row,' said Moss, 'where that big tree came down in spring.'

'Oh yes, we remember,' said Squeak. 'Thank Pan nobody we know was hibernating in it! That would have been a tragedy.'

'Excuse me, but it *was* a tragedy! Me and Moss were fast asleep in the hollow trunk,' chipped in Burnet.

'Oh, I'm terribly sorry. Had you been staying there long?'

'Hundreds of cuckoo summers. It was – it was our home.'

'Oh. Well, I'm afraid it's not there any more,' squeaked Pip, still circling above them. 'The Mortals cut it all up and took it away, even the stump, and then they filled in the hole where its roots grew. It's just lawn now, smooth and green, with hardly anything living in it, as though an ash tree never even grew there at all.'

Burnet and Moss looked at one another, stricken. It was so sad to think that the last of the row of ancient ash trees was now gone, with nothing to show it had ever been there.

'Well, we need to get to the garden anyway,' said Moss. 'Between you two and Spangle, can you keep us safe from cats as we cross town?'

'Absolutely.'

'Are you sure?' said Moss. 'It's just that – well, the thing is, I was caught by one a while ago, and I'm still really scared.'

'Trust us. We may only be tiny, but we've got your backs.'

They set off along the footpath that led from the river to the houses, Spangle hopping from branch to branch above them and calling down directions in a loud whisper, the two pipistrelles fluttering somewhere above them, acting as lookouts. Street-lights lit the way; although Pip and Squeak checked to see if any moths were fluttering around them, it was the time of year when flying insects become scarce.

Moss gazed at all the lights in the terraced houses they passed: the flickering bluish light from TVs in front rooms with their blinds closed, and the warmer yellow glow from curtained upstairs rooms where children were reading, or being read to, or settling down under their duvets by the faint gleam of a nightlight.

'Does any of this feel familiar?' asked Sorrel. 'We can't be too far away now.'

'I don't recognize anything yet,' said Moss.

'No, all these houses were built long after me and Moss set up home in the ash tree,' said Burnet.

'Back then it was all fields with sheep in – oh, and that nice old wooden farmhouse down the muddy lane.'

'Funny to think Ash Row became part of the Hive's outskirts, isn't it?' said Moss. 'We had no idea! I mean, we knew lots of buildings had been built over the fields, and that there were more and more Mortals living around us, but we didn't realize the margins of the Hive had swallowed us up.'

They came to the end of the street, passed a big church and turned a corner to find a wide precinct lined with shops. There weren't any Mortals about, but the window displays still had lights on, which seemed very surprising to the Hidden Folk.

'I know, it's so confusing for all the Night People,' squeaked Pip from somewhere above. 'I'd much rather live somewhere darker, wouldn't you, Squeak?'

'*And* it confuses the birds,' Squeak agreed. 'No wonder they sometimes sing at night, poor dears.'

Dormer was carefully scanning the shopping precinct. There weren't many places to take cover, or where they could hurry along in shadow, unseen.

'We just have to risk it. Let's take it as fast as we can. But we've got to stick together, all right?'

The others nodded.

'Do you want to hold my hand, Moss?' asked Burnet.

'Yes, please.'

Dormer led the way. Tiny as mice, they scuttled past several clothes shops, a pharmacy, a shoe shop and a bookshop (which, as everyone knows, is the best kind of shop), before coming to a charity shop which had two big bags of donated toys and clothes by its door, ready to be taken inside in the morning. Dormer nipped smartly behind the bags, and they all paused for breath.

'Where now, Spangle?'

'Cross the road, cut through the huge big children's building, round the corner, then you're home. Well, *you* ain't, Dormer, but you know what I mean.'

'Have we got time to look through these bags for anything useful?' asked Sorrel, hopefully.

'No!' said the others, all at the same time.

The road was wide, and, although it was night, a few death-chariots still rumbled along in both directions: there were ordinary ones, and taxis, and even a night bus. To the left, the road went around a corner and it was hard to see what was coming from that direction, or how fast.

'So what you do is, you wait for a gap and then you just run across as fast as you can,' said Burnet.

'Actually . . .' said Dormer.

'That's what I did when we travelled with the deer, and it worked ever so well. Didn't it, everyone?'

And with that, Burnet began marching off towards the kerb.

'Psst! Wait!' cried Dormer. 'Come back, it's not safe!'

'What?'

'It's just that . . . well, there's another way to do it. I learnt about it in the Hive. See those big sticks with lights on, and that stripy bit on the ground? Every so often those lights will go red, all the death-chariots will stop as if by Pan's command, there'll be a *beep beep beep* sound, and then you can just walk across.'

'But – won't the death-chariots be able to see us prancing along in front of them?'

'The trick is to go behind.'

So that's what they did: they waited until the traffic lights went red and the pelican crossing started to beep, and then they crossed the road behind the cars that had drawn up. One driver did glance in his rear-view mirror, but all he saw were a few scudding leaves on the tarmac, and nobody suspected a thing.

'Woo-hoo!' said Dormer, and high-fived everybody.

'Nice one,' called Spangle.

'Good work!' squeaked the bats.

When they came to the fence enclosing the school playground, Spangle perched on top while the four Hidden Folk slipped easily through the gaps. Then Pip and Squeak circled lower and lower before latching on to the fence with their feet and hanging upside-down above the four, so they could all talk easily.

'Right, you lot: this is the home stretch,' said Spangle. 'On the other side of this building, whatever it is, is the end of Ash Row. Walk down the street and you'll find your old garden. Pip, Squeak – you ready? I've done a bit of a recce and there could be cats about.'

'We're ready,' said Pip. 'We're going to flap right in the face of anything that comes near you – both of us together!'

'*Flap-flap-flap-flap-flap!* Take that, meanies!' added Squeak, excitedly.

'I can't believe we're almost home, after all our adventures,' said Moss. 'I just wish Cumulus was with us – don't you, Burnet?'

Burnet nodded. 'It does feel really strange. But you know what? Cumulus would want us to carry on with our mission, so that's what we're going to do.'

The four set out in single file around the edge of the playground, sticking close to the school walls. The windows were dark, but a single light burnt above the main entrance, casting their shadows on the ground. Sorrel was momentarily distracted by a hopscotch game painted on the tarmac, and wanted to investigate; quickly, and with a great deal of shushing, the others dragged their friend away.

They rounded a corner and scuttled past the big double doors. Then they dashed to a set of benches, paused under one to catch their breath, and, encouraged by Spangle in a loud whisper, ran, crouching, past a big climbing frame.

They were nearly across the playground, the other fence in sight, when it happened. A dark shape appeared suddenly out of some bushes, and immediately the bats dived, uttering high-pitched, war-like shrieks. Moss screamed and grabbed Burnet, who tried to stand firm; in the darkness it was impossible to know what direction they were being attacked from, so they huddled protectively around Moss, sheltering their heads. For a few moments the world was a kerfuffle of dark wings as Spangle dived to join in the fray, his frantic beeps and expletives adding to the confusion.

And then, as quickly as it had started, the fight

was over: there was a shout, the two bats broke away to cling to the fence, and Spangle sprang back in surprise. And there before them on the tarmac of the school playground they saw not a cat, or even a kitten, but an unfamiliar, and furious-looking, member of the Hidden Folk.

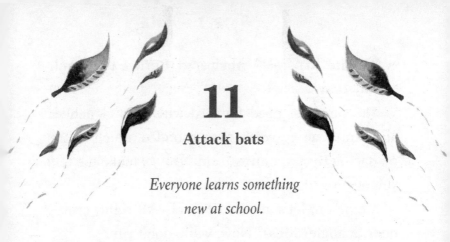

11

Attack bats

*Everyone learns something
new at school.*

A round hunter's moon shone coldly down on the school playground, where Moss, Burnet, Sorrel and Dormer gazed open-mouthed at the black-clad figure in front of them, who glared angrily back.

'Go on, get lost!' snarled the little person. 'And take your . . . your *attack bats* with you, and that flea-ridden starling too! This is my territory, and you're not welcome here.'

'Oi, who are you calling flea-ridden?' chirped Spangle, puffing out his feathers and standing tall. Moss's heart thumped; people shouting always felt scary.

'I said, get lost!' the stranger shouted. 'Or I'll set the rats on you, and, believe me, you do *not* want that!'

'I quite like rats,' whispered Burnet to Sorrel. 'Always have.'

The figure stepped forward with fists clenched, and, in a quiet voice that sounded much more menacing than shouting, said, 'Do *not* make me tell you again.'

'Come on, let's go,' said Sorrel. 'All right, everyone? Spangle? Moss? Now, walk, don't run.'

Slowly they all backed away together until they reached the fence where the bats were waiting for them. They slipped through, one by one, to the street beyond – and then ran behind one of the big grey wheelie bins that guarded each house like towering Easter Island heads (it was bin night for Mortalkind). As Squeak and Pip circled overhead, Sorrel was the first to speak.

'Well, I never. *Well – I – never.* All that time you lived here, and there were Hidden Folk right at the end of your street!'

'I can't believe it!' said Moss. 'Can you, Burnet?'

'Why didn't anyone tell us,' replied Burnet, 'like Mr B the blackbird, for example? You would have thought he'd have known.'

'Or, more to the point, a certain starling?' said Moss, turning to Spangle. 'I mean, you used to come here all the time – you were always talking about the food the children dropped!'

'Swear down, Bosses, I never knew! You think I'd have let you go off on an entire quest-based-adventure to find more of your lot without mentioning that particular nugget of info? Give me *some* credit.'

'Fair enough,' replied Moss. 'And anyway, whoever that was didn't seem very sociable. Probably not the type to get out and about much.'

'I suppose we did set two attack bats on them,' said Burnet. 'I'd have probably been a bit cross, too.'

Dormer spoke up. 'You know, I've got a feeling . . . I think that might have been a Hob.'

'Oh, that's interesting,' said Sorrel. 'What makes you say so?'

'Well, it's hard to be sure, but . . . I think those black clothes were made of something unnatural, something Mortal-made. Didn't anyone else notice?'

'I didn't,' said Moss.

'Nor me,' said Burnet.

'Now you mention it, I think I know what you mean!' said Sorrel. 'Kind of shiny, and waterproof . . . I feel like I've seen that stuff before.'

'I bet you could make friends with them if you tried, Dormer,' said Moss. 'For one thing, you're really good at it. You made me feel like we'd known each other for ages, about six seconds after we'd met!'

But there was no time to discuss it further. 'Excuse me,' came Squeak's high voice from above. 'D'you still need us, or are you all right from here? Only Pip just heard some gnats hatching out in a distant compost heap.'

'Safe,' said Spangle. 'I mean, there's only one cat at this end of the street and it's got a very tinkly bell, so we literally will be safe.'

'Oh, brilliant – that's a relief!' called Pip. 'Well, it was nice to meet you, elves! Do keep in touch.'

'Wait!' called Moss. 'Before you go – did you say you were about to hibernate?'

'Yes, we tend to when all the insects have run out for the year,' said Squeak. 'Depends how many gnats we find tonight, I suppose, and whether the temperature drops. Why?'

'Oh, just . . . could you wait a few more nights, maybe? Say three? But if you haven't heard from us by then, feel free to sleep, obviously.'

'Well, we can try, depending on the weather,' came the high-pitched voice. 'Can't we, Pip?'

'Can't promise anything, especially as there's bad weather coming . . . but we'll do our best! Bye for now! Bye! *Byeeeeeeeeeeeeee!*'

After the bats had disappeared over the roofs of the houses, Dormer looked at Moss quizzically. 'What was that about?'

'Oh, nothing,' said Moss. 'Just an idea I've had.'

'Right,' said Spangle. 'You lot ready? Only six Mortal houses to pass and then we're there.'

'It's so strange, I don't remember any of this,' said Burnet, peeping out from behind the bin. 'But at the same time, I can *feel* that we're close somehow.'

'Homing instinct,' said Spangle. 'Us birds get it really strongly. As for why you don't recognize anything, you went the other way down the street when you left. This is the top end.'

'Ah, that makes sense.'

With that, the four friends stepped cautiously out from behind the wheelie bin and, keeping to the inside of the pavement, slipped quietly along Ash Row in the dark. Moss was momentarily distracted by a carved pumpkin that had been left outside someone's gate and smelt delicious; meanwhile, the parked death-chariots were very interesting to Sorrel, who made a mental note to come back and look another time – as long as the huge machines were all asleep, as they seemed to be now. They passed bin after bin, and, at one point, a big white sign with six black symbols on it, in two groups of three. The legs of the sign smelt strongly of dog wee, and they hurried on.

Spangle was fluttering back and forth ahead, perching now on a garden wall and now on the lower branches of a street tree, all the while keeping a beady eye on their surroundings. From his vantage point, he saw the exact moment when it clicked for Moss and Burnet, and they recognized exactly where they were.

Burnet stopped dead, and the others did, too. After gazing down one of the little paths that led between the houses to their back gardens, Burnet turned to Moss, and the two held hands. Sorrel and Dormer fell back a little, to let the friends have a moment to themselves.

'This is it, Moss,' whispered Burnet. 'Home at last. How do you feel?'

'A bit nervous, to tell you the truth,' said Moss. 'I've been trying to prepare myself for our tree not being there any more, but I don't know whether I've managed it or not.'

'Me either,' replied Burnet. 'Our poor, homely old ash.'

Moss squeezed Burnet's hand. 'Come on, we'll do it together – all right?'

And so the two led the way down the side of the house, past the drains and the bin area and under the garden gate to the dear old garden they'd thought they might never see again.

YEW

12

Home sweet home?

Back at Ash Row,
there are surprises in store.

The planets Venus and Mercury, and the dazzling star Arcturus, were fading in the light of the slowly rising sun as millions of miles across the galaxy two Earth-dwelling Hidden Folk named Moss and Burnet stood and gazed at the garden they'd once lived in so happily, and for so long. Behind them stood their dear friends Dormer and Sorrel, while a cheeky starling named Spangle perched on the fence and for once kept his beak shut. It was an important moment for everyone.

'It's . . . it's like our tree was never even there,' whispered Burnet, at last.

'You'd hardly think it was the same garden,' replied Moss. 'Look at all that that smooth green lawn, with no fallen ash leaves on it at all!'

Burnet squeezed Moss's hand with one invisible

one. 'How are you doing, dear friend? Are you all right?'

'Do you know, I think I feel a bit . . . relieved, in a way. It almost looks like a different garden, and that's easier. And at least we don't have to look at our home all smashed up and broken.'

'That's true.'

'Where was it?' said Sorrel, and Moss pointed out the place in the corner, near the trampoline.

'I remember when this was all fields,' mused Burnet.

'Yes, you see, when we first lived here, hundreds of cuckoo summers ago, our ash was one in a row of trees in a hedge,' explained Moss. 'And there were sheep in the fields all around us. I liked them.'

'Come on, let's have a look around and see what's what,' said Burnet, and led the way into the tangled flower bed, which looked so familiar and yet so unfamiliar at the same time. They had missed a whole season's growth and a whole summer's flowers: everything was over now, so it was hard to tell how it had looked in full bloom or what exactly had grown where – especially as the first frosts had killed off a lot of the more delicate plants so they were dead and brown. Yet under their feet, as they walked, lay thousands of tiny seeds and thousands of sleeping roots, ready to burst into life next spring.

'I wonder if any of the Garden People are awake,' said Burnet. 'Mr B the blackbird, or Whiskers, for instance. The mouse clan are busy at night; he might still be up and about.'

'Or Carlos - he's an early riser,' said Moss, before explaining to the others about the troupe of bright green parakeets that had only arrived recently, and how much fun they had turned out to be.

'Oh yes, there were some of those near where I lived, in the Hive. They might have been Carlos's cousins, in fact!' Dormer said.

They reached the evergreen laurel bush Moss and Burnet had sheltered under so many times in the past and paused to regroup. Spangle fluttered down to join them and snapped up an unfortunate worm who had just broken ground to see if there were any wet leaves for breakfast.

'Early bird and all that,' the starling chirped, and then, 'Ooh, no wonder she came to the surface. Feels like rain, that does.'

He was right: it had begun to rain lightly, the kind of dull, persistent drizzle that can soak you to the skin. The Hidden Folk huddled together under the shrub, but soon drops of water began to slide off the leaves above them and fall on them, each landing with a wet, cold plop.

'Shall we pitch our tents?' suggested Sorrel, who was shivering. 'I could do with a rest – we've been walking all night.'

Burnet stepped out from under the laurel and peered up at the sky. 'This weather is set in, I'd say – there are no patches of blue sky, and no breeze to move the rain clouds on. I think Sorrel's right: we might as well wait it out.'

'I've got a better idea,' said Spangle. 'Just gonna check something' – and he fluttered over the fence into the garden of 51 Ash Row, returning thirty seconds later, looking triumphant.

'Right, let's go next door – I've got the perfect spot for you to kip. I am an actual genius sometimes, if I do say so myself.'

'Next door?' said Moss. 'But – *this* is our garden, not that one.'

'I know, Boss, but do you really fancy camping out in a flower bed in the rain?'

Moss looked at Dormer, who shrugged. 'Perhaps he's right, Moss. Anyway, haven't you ever been curious about what's on the other side of the fence?'

'*I* certainly have,' said Burnet. 'We should have done a recce when the tree smashed down the fence, but we were too shocked, and then there was so much to do to get ready to leave. But, Spangle, how will we get into next-door's garden now that the fence has been repaired?'

'Oh, that's easy,' said Sorrel. 'There's a plant growing up it over there – look! We can just use it like a climbing frame.'

'That never used to be there,' said Moss, doubtfully. Now that the initial shock of seeing the garden without the ash tree was over, all the other, smaller changes were starting to add up, and it felt very strange.

'I expect the Mortals are hoping it'll grow and hide that new-looking fence panel,' said Dormer. 'That's the kind of thing they do.'

They all trooped over to the plant. It was a young clematis, and earlier in the year it had had big purple flowers, but now all that was left of them were some fluffy seed heads covered in glistening droplets of rain. Its twisting stems were tied to a wooden trellis that had been fixed to the fence – an added benefit.

Spangle flew to the top of the fence and peered down at them, watching their progress. Burnet went first, shinning easily up the clematis stem and using its side shoots as handholds. The others tightened the straps of their backpacks, and Sorrel made sure that the hood of the frogskin onesie wouldn't fall forward like it sometimes did and make it hard to see.

'See you at the top!' Burnet called, from halfway up the fence.

Sorrel went next, checking that each clematis tendril was strong enough before clambering up to the next one, and Moss and Dormer followed. The bars of the trellis, when they could reach them, provided the best and most stable hand- and foot-holds, and before long all four of them were sitting on top of the fence, getting wet bums and dangling their feet into next-door's garden.

'Wow,' said Dormer, who knew a bit about Mortal gardens, but had never seen anything as interesting as this one before.

'I know, right?' cheeped Spangle, bobbing his head up and down and looking smug.

'It's amazing!' said Sorrel. 'Do you think they're inventors? Surely they must be.'

The garden next door was completely different to the one they'd lived in for so long. There wasn't any lawn, for one thing. Instead it looked as though, in summer, the end of the garden had been a wild-flower area, its tall grass brown now, but with the seed heads of lots of different plants and flowers still in it. Drizzle was dimpling the surface of a pond, which had vegetation growing all around it, and there were tangly bits where all sorts of different plants grew thickly together, creating excellent places to hide. There were bug hotels here and there, a compost heap, a log pile, a bird table with feeders hanging from it, and a water butt to collect rainwater, and through it all wound interesting-looking paths for the Mortals who lived there to walk along, and smaller paths too, made by animals. It looked like a brilliant place for wild creatures of all kinds to live.

'Can you even *imagine* what that must have looked like in spring?' asked Burnet. 'I bet it was amazing! Bees and butterflies everywhere, frogs and newts in the pond, caterpillars for the baby birds to eat, loads of flying insects for the Air People, like the swallows and house martins and swifts and bats . . .'

'Oh yeah, you should've seen it,' agreed Spangle. 'I mean, you and Moss *really* should've, being right next door.'

'I just wish Cumulus was here,' said Moss, sadly.

'One day soon we'll all be visible again, and then we'll be reunited,' Burnet replied, in a voice that

113

sounded more certain than any of them felt. 'And Cumulus will *love* this place.'

'Anyway, point is, I've got just the place for you to bed down for now. Take your pick!' Spangle gestured with his beak.

And that's when they saw the nest boxes, some plain and sturdy, some smaller and daubed with bright sploshes of paint. There were boxes with small entrance holes and boxes with bigger holes, open-fronted ones, pyramidal ones and teardrop-shaped ones. They were fixed to the fences, to the shed, to trees and bushes, and even under the eaves of the house.

'They're for us lot really, but nobody'll mind you making use of a few in your hour of need,' explained the starling. 'Personally, I'd go for them ones underneath us. They're for sparrows, which is why there's four together – they get lonely otherwise.'

Moss, Dormer, Burnet and Sorrel looked down. Just below their dangling feet, they saw the roofs of four nest boxes fixed to the fence. Straight away, Burnet jumped down to land on top of one, then peered carefully over the edge before disappearing, head-first. After a moment there came a muffled shout from inside the box: 'This is the best thing *ever*! I call dibs on this one!' At which point the others all followed suit.

For a few minutes, banging and thumping could be heard from the four nest boxes on the fence of 51 Ash Row as each of the Hidden Folk moved in and got settled. Every so often a bit of old nest was pushed from one of the entrance holes, or a dead louse was flung out with a shout of 'Yuck!' Moss, in particular, wanted to get everything clean and tidy, so dust, bits of twig, fragments of eggshell and old feathers came flying out of the box nearest the house and drifted to the ground. They were all so busy, and were making so much noise, that none of them noticed Spangle's extra-loud, repeated alarm call, or the fact that he had flown off from his perch on the fence.

Instead, they called cheerily to one another through the wooden walls, describing the interiors of their respective nest boxes and boasting about which was the best – especially Burnet. So it came as a shock to find, when at last they all poked their heads out of the entrance holes to talk properly, that in front of them stood a Mortal child, with her hands in the pockets of her dungarees and a great big frown on her face.

13

First contact

They say it's good to talk –
but not everyone is
happy to.

'Well,' said Ro, speaking the Wild Argot as naturally as any wild creature. 'You aren't sparrows, and these boxes are meant especially for them, which means that, technically, you're trespassing, which means that, technically, I should get my dad, except I'm not going to because of "Live and Let Live", which is a rule that means be nice to people if they're not doing any harm, which I suppose you're not, technically. And also I'm not going to because you're Moss, and I remember you from before. Hello.'

The last time Ro had spoken to them, Moss had been too shocked and scared to reply. Their ash-tree home had just come crashing down after a storm, none of them knew what had happened, and, anyway, the idea of a Mortal speaking the Wild

116

Argot was too bizarre to be believed. But since then, there'd been time to think and plan and prepare for meeting her again, even if it was happening a little bit sooner than expected. Making friends with her was crucial, because, without the aid of Mortals, the Hidden Folk knew deep down that it would be hard to help the Wild World. The fact was, Ro held the key to saving Cumulus, if such a thing was still possible – and to Moss it was dear old Cumulus who mattered most.

Summoning all the courage learnt from every step of their adventures, every challenge, every setback, every triumph, big and small, Moss took a deep breath, and, in the most important speech any of them had ever made in all their long lives, said:

'Hello.'

'So you *can* speak. That's good. And why exactly are you in my bird boxes?'

'Erm, well, it's just that . . .' began Moss.

'Well?'

'Spangle said we could stay here, and . . .'

'Who's Spangle?'

'A bird. Well, a starling.'

'I do see a starling in my garden every so often, but I didn't know he had a name. Do all the birds and animals have names, then?'

'Er—' began Moss, a bit surprised by the question.

'Do all Mortals?' interrupted Sorrel.

'Course we do!'

'*Well*, then!'

'So . . . what are your names, then?' asked Ro. 'I mean, I know you're called Moss, and that it isn't short for anything. What about the rest of you?'

'Burnet,' said Burnet loudly and firmly, in the kind of voice that's supposed to sound brave.

'I'm Sorrel,' said Sorrel.

'D-Dormer,' came a quavery voice from the last box in the row. 'H-h-hello.'

'Nice to meet you all. I'm Ro, and this is my garden. You can live here if you like. I've decided it's OK.'

'Thank you very much,' said Moss, and the others all thanked her, too. It was amazing how brave they were all being – at least for now, anyway. Nobody had screamed or fainted, though of course they couldn't wait to talk it through with each other properly, once Ro had gone. As well as being one of the most extraordinary moments of their lives, it was a historic turning point in Mortal-Hidden Folk relations, one that would be remembered by both species for ever and ever and – who knows? – might even go on to change the world.

'So . . . how come you can speak the Wild Argot?' asked Moss, curiously.

'The what?'

'The Wild Argot – the language of animals.'

'Oh! I didn't realize I could. It just . . . sort of came to me. I thought I was talking normally.'

'You are! I mean, you're talking normally for us. Have you spoken to any of the other Garden People?'

'No,' said Ro, sadly. 'They never come close enough. It's like everything's scared of me, I don't know why. I'm a very kind person, actually. You can ask anyone who really knows me, or even my dad if you want.'

'And . . . are you the only one?'

'The only one what?'

'The only one of your kind who can speak the Wild Argot.'

'Oh! I dunno really. I hope so – that would be cool. I definitely don't think Maya or Ben can. They live next door. What *are* you?'

'Pardon?' said Moss, who was finding it a bit hard to keep up.

'Like, there are birds and mammals and reptiles and amphibians and insects and crustaceans and fish. But what are *you*?'

'Oh, I see! Well, we're Hidden Folk. We've been in the world since for ever, but not many of your kind have seen us – or believe in us, for that matter.'

'I do,' said Ro. 'I can see you, for one thing. And anyway, it makes sense.'

'How do you mean?'

Ro shrugged. 'There are so many stories about fairies and gnomes and pixies, and I knew not to believe in them, but . . . I felt like there must be a *reason* for all the stories, even if you didn't exist any more. Even if you'd disappeared a long time ago.'

'About that,' began Moss, quickly trying to think of the best way to explain what was happening to them – but just then there came a shout from inside the house. None of the Hidden Folk could understand it, of course, but Ro could, and after shouting back in Mortal language she said, 'Sorry, Hidden Folks: got to go. Dad's made breakfast, and then we're going to visit my auntie – it's half-term, did you know? But I'll come and see you tomorrow morning, OK? Bye for now!'

And with that she ran inside, and was gone.

Immediately there came the scratchy sound of bird feet on the fence above them, as Spangle landed and let out a torrent of clicks and whistles and explosive-sounding beeps, many of which were untranslatable avian curses but which eventually resolved into the spluttered question, *What in the whole Wild World did they actually think they were doing, talking to a complete and utter Mortal like that?*

'Look, we can't talk properly, all in our separate boxes like this,' said Burnet. 'Has everyone got a bit of line for fishing? Good. Knot it to the perch under the entrance hole, use it to rappel to the ground, and then we can have a proper talk.'

Moments later the four Hidden Folk were down in the damp and tangled shrubbery. Spangle joined them, his feathers sticking out at odd angles with fright.

'Now look: I know what you're going to say, Spangle,' said Moss, 'but you know we need a new job if we're to stay in the Wild World, and it's going to take more than just picking up litter. The second of Robin Goodfellow's teachings was that Mortals will one day be our friends – don't you remember what Cumulus said? And Ro's a Mortal who speaks the Wild Argot, and she seems really kind. If our job now is to save the Wild World, she's the Mortal who can help us. She can be our first friend.'

'*Friend?*' spluttered Spangle. 'Pan alive, you gotta be kidding me.'

'We can't build nest boxes, can we?' Moss went on. 'Or dig ponds, or stop Mortals poisoning the flowers the bees and butterflies rely on. But if we find out what the Garden People next door need, Ro can tell the Mortals that live there, and they'll do it.'

'*Why* will they do it?' said Spangle. 'The Mortals, I mean.'

'Well . . . to be helpful, of course!' replied Moss. 'Everyone likes to be helpful. Don't they?'

'Not sure about that, Boss, if I'm brutally honest. And anyway, why should they listen to her? She's only a kid.'

Sometimes you hold on to a plan in your head for ages, and it seems like a good one, but when you tell someone else, it seems to shrivel up like a punctured balloon. That's how Spangle's reaction made Moss feel: deflated.

'But what's the alternative, Spangle?' Dormer interjected. 'Just . . . try to make next-door's garden better all by ourselves? Plant a few wildflower seeds? Hand-pollinate some blossom? Help the mason bees find nest holes? It doesn't seem enough, if you ask me: not if we really want to show Pan we're still useful, and that we deserve to stay in the Wild World.'

'Listen up,' said Spangle impatiently. 'I know you lot've all got a bumblebee in your best bonnets about finding a job and all that, and it's not good enough for you to live like the rest of us, just trying to get by. You think being useful will stop you from fading away. But the truth is this: we're *all* fading away – or most of us, anyway. Us starlings, we know it. There used to be clouds of my kind in the sky in autumn and winter, and now you barely see six of us together. Sparrows: same. Stag beetles. Butterflies. And tell me when any of you last saw a hedgehog. You ain't special. We're *all* disappearing. And there's not a *bleeping* thing any wild creature can do about it.'

Everyone looked shocked – even Spangle, who had been keeping that painful thought to himself for a long time, and hadn't planned to say it out loud.

'Look, I'm sorry,' the little starling continued, his voice cracking as he dropped his sleek head. 'I don't mean to discourage you. You know I loved Cumulus like a brother, and all this time I've had your backs. But you've just shown yourselves to a Mortal, and now you're thinking of trusting them with all our secrets and our problems – things we've always tried to keep hidden and out of Mortal sight!

How do you know it's not going to make things worse?'

'I – I don't, to be honest,' said Moss, hesitatingly. 'But we need Mortal help to do this properly, and Ro and her dad are already doing good things in their garden. I think we should trust them.'

'Absolutely *no way* am I speaking to her dad, or any adult Mortal,' said Spangle, wagging his beak from side to side. 'Red line. No way. Not happening. Jog on.'

'I've got an idea,' said Dormer. 'What if we make that a rule? No grown-up Mortals ever get to see us or talk to us – just children. I've been living alongside Mortals for a long time now, and I can promise you that some of the young ones are lovely. Not all, granted, but some.'

'But how d'you know which ones can be trusted and which ones can't?' asked Spangle.

'We don't, but Ro might,' said Burnet. 'Stop worrying, Spangle – it'll be *fine.*'

Despite Burnet's support, Moss was starting to feel really unsure about their plan. 'This is all going a bit fast, isn't it? I didn't think we'd run into Ro so quickly, and I forgot Spangle hadn't been told about this part of the plan. I'm not sure about it all now.'

'Now I think about it, a lot of our conversations

about it happened indoors, at Mac and Min's place,' said Sorrel.

'Well, now you know . . . do you really think it's a bad idea, Spangle?' asked Moss.

'Ain't no love lost between starlings and Mortals,' said the starling. 'They've hated us for years, Pan only knows why, so I don't trust 'em. That's the angle I'm coming from – and I don't think I'm the only one who'll say the same.'

'I was thinking,' said Moss. 'What if we got all the Garden People together?'

'Ooh, like a party?' said Burnet.

'Not . . . exactly,' said Moss. 'More like a conference. Bob and Roberta the blackbirds, and Carlos the parakeet and his tribe, the house mice, Olivia and Whiskers. And all the moths and beetles, sparrows, voles, spiders, toads, grass snakes – *everything*. Let's get them all in one place so we can decide together. Sharing our problems with Mortal children is too big a decision to make on our own.'

14

The conference

*An important matter
is put to the vote.*

Spangle was given the job of telling everyone about the grand conference of all the animals – not just the Garden People from 51 and 52 Ash Row, but the entire neighbourhood. The plan was for each species to send no more than two representatives so the gathering wouldn't be overrun with creatures there were a lot of, like earwigs; as for how those two should be chosen, Spangle wisely decided not to get involved, but to simply spread the news.

'What about the summer birds?' asked Moss. 'They've all migrated to warmer countries for the winter. And what about the grasshoppers and butterflies? At this time of year they're either eggs or pupae – they won't hatch out until next spring.'

'Look, it isn't going to be perfect,' said Dormer,

sensibly. 'But it's the best we can do right now. We can't just make decisions for everyone. We need to make sure as many creatures as possible are on side.'

'Dormer's right,' said Sorrel. 'But first, I need a nap – don't you? I'm exhausted. Let's climb back up our ropes and curl up in our nest boxes for a while.'

By about teatime the rain clouds had moved away. Burnet got up first and went back next door with Sorrel to dig up the supplies they'd buried all those months ago, and then they all changed into their warm winter clothes and had a good meal of acorn bread and nut butter, which keeps for ages as long as it's properly stored.

One by one the lights came on in the houses as a cold red sun set slowly in the west. The Hidden Folk gathered in the garden's wildflower patch to wait as the last rays of light slowly faded, and the air grew chilly. Dormer suggested lighting a fire, but Burnet said it didn't seem like a good idea among all the dead grass, even if it was still damp from the morning's rain.

'I've just thought,' said Moss, who was shivering a little. 'Are we going to sleep through the winter, like we usually do?'

'That's a good question,' said Burnet. 'I wonder

what would happen if we didn't? I mean, we can't just clock off for three months in the middle of saving the Wild World, can we?'

'Do you know, I've always wanted to know what the cold part of the year is actually like,' mused Sorrel.

'What if it's really scary?' said Moss. 'There must be a reason we always sleep through it. What if terrifying things happen in winter that we don't know about?'

'Or maybe us sleeping through it was just a tradition,' said Burnet. 'Traditions are all very well, but they can change.'

Dormer was about to tell them that Hobs don't sleep through winter, because they live indoors and don't need to, but just then a glossy brown and gold frog hopped through the grass stems. 'Oh,' she said. 'Am I the first? I hate being the first to arrive at a party. Also, I was told there would be snacks.'

'Hello,' said Burnet. 'No snacks – sorry. Are you on your own?'

'Couldn't find anyone else – they're all hibernating early, I expect, the lazy so-and-sos. I'm Cora. And who are you?'

'Burnet, and we're Hidden Folk. This is Moss, and . . .'

Just as Burnet was about to do the introductions, more creatures began to arrive. First came Bob and Roberta the blackbirds, who were thrilled to see Moss and Burnet again. Then the entire house-mouse clan arrived, all seven of them, because they couldn't bear to be separated. There were two each of wood pigeons, urban pigeons and their cousins, the shy collared doves; a pair of young foxes, who turned out to be distant cousins of Vesper's; Carlos and Juanita the green parakeets; four questing voles (two bank and two field) and three hyperactive shrews (two common and one pygmy); several grumpy earthworms, still bearing a grudge against Burnet; Spink the chaffinch, and his partner, Buff; a couple of slow-worms; a family of grey squirrels; Sven the grass snake, who happened to be nearby and hadn't managed to hibernate yet; Spuggie and Phip, the matriarch and patriarch of the sparrow gang; and assorted slugs, snails, centipedes, ants, spiders and other small beasts. From one tree hung Pip and Squeak the bats, while in another perched a couple of magpies and a male and female sparrowhawk, who were trying very hard not to make all the smaller birds nervous, mostly without success. At the very last moment, Spangle flew in and perched on the fence next to Carlos and Juanita.

'Right, then,' said Burnet, who, as the oldest, felt some responsibility to kick things off. 'We are gathered here today to discuss the Mortal child known as Ro, and—'

'Why are you not, er, *all there?*' came a deep voice from the back.

'Yeah, that's what I want to know too,' shouted someone else.

'Oh, er – well, it's a long story . . .'

'Best hurry up, then,' said the first voice, which turned out to belong to a wood pigeon.

'Are there definitely no snacks?' asked Cora, as chatter began to rise from all the assorted animals.

Burnet felt things were fast getting out of hand, and shot Moss a slightly desperate look.

'Say something!' whispered Dormer, with an encouraging nudge. 'You're good with words, and you know lots of these creatures. You can do it.'

Feeling nervous but determined, Moss stood up and faced the assorted animals.

'Thank you so much for coming, old friends and new. It's really kind of you all, and we appreciate the trouble you've gone to,' Moss began. 'We asked you to come today because – well, we need your help.'

Everyone fell silent. They could tell from Moss's voice that it was important, and they all felt it was nice to be thanked. Some had come a long way, and some had braved serious dangers, like roads; as well as that, many were in closer proximity to the creatures that usually ate them than they otherwise would have liked.

'We're Hidden Folk,' Moss went on, 'and a long time ago it was our job to take care of the Wild World. Some of you know me and Burnet from when we lived next door, others may have heard of our kind in old stories and legends, but for many of you, this may be the first time you've come across us, because there are fewer and fewer of us these days – just like there are fewer of many of you, too.

'It seems that our kind aren't needed any more, and so we're fading out of the Wild World – that's what's happening to Burnet here, and to Sorrel; and soon it'll start happening to me and Dormer, too. In a little while there'll be none of us left, and, just like the dinosaurs or the Large Copper butterfly, we'll never, *ever* exist again.

'But there's a way to stop this from happening, and it won't just help us – it'll help all of you, too. We believe that if we find a way to be useful, Pan will stop us from fading away – and maybe our dear friend Cumulus will come back. Now, I know you won't believe this, but there's a Mortal child in that house who speaks the Wild Argot, which is why we've returned to Ash Row. I trust her, and I think we should ask for her help to save the Wild World. But only if you all agree.'

'Ask Mortals to help us?' came the harsh cry of Musket the male sparrowhawk from up in the tree. 'What in the name of Pan are you talking about?'

'But they already do!' said Moss. 'Just look at this garden: it's got *loads* more creatures living in it than all the others, hasn't it?'

'Like . . . in our boxes, for instance?' chirped Spuggie. When Moss looked embarrassed, she continued, more kindly, 'Don't worry, we're roosting in the ivy right now.'

'It's true there are loads more insects to eat in this garden,' said Squeak the bat.

'I have to say, I do love that pond,' said Cora, fondly. 'I've raised many a tadpole there.'

'*Very tathty*,' Sven hissed quietly to himself.

'Well, imagine next-door's garden, where we used to live, was as welcoming to wild creatures as this one,' said Moss, 'and the one next to that, and the one next to that. And imagine if they could be even better! What kind of things would you want?'

'Unlimited worms!' chirped Bob.

'We can hear you, you know,' muttered one of the worms. 'So rude.'

'Fewer blackbirds!' shouted another worm, excitedly.

'More voles!' barked one of the foxes.

'No foxes allowed!' squeaked one of the voles.

'I can see this getting complicated,' muttered Sorrel.

'I probably shouldn't have asked that,' admitted Moss.

'Let's just slow down and focus on one thing at a time,' said Dormer, who could see that Moss was starting to look upset. 'All we need to know right now is whether you Garden People trust us to be your representatives. Everything else we can work out later on. We Hidden Folk have all looked after special places before: we know how to do it, and it's something we can teach Mortalkind. But for now, let's decide whether to trust Ro, and take it from there.'

'I think that's very sensible,' said Burnet. 'Shall we have a vote? How about . . . everyone in favour of us talking to Mortals stands on *this* side, and everyone who thinks we shouldn't involve them stands over *there*.'

'Where?' squawked Carlos.

133

'Psst, Burnet, you've got no *arms*,' hissed Sorrel.

'Oh! Sorry. Give us a hand, Sorrel, will you? Preferably your visible one.'

Between them, Sorrel and Burnet managed to indicate to the assembled animals which side meant a 'yes' vote and which side meant 'no'. And then there was a short burst of confusion as everyone ran, shuffled, flapped or hopped into place, and a small hillock of earth appeared on the 'yes' side, thrown up by a mole nobody had known was there.

At the end of it, it was clear to everyone that there were more votes in favour of talking to Ro than against. But as Moss and Dormer hugged, and Burnet got talking to Bob and Roberta the black-birds, Sorrel happened to glance into the shadows and there, on the 'no' side, behind Spangle, stood a small, black-clad figure with folded arms.

15

A broken heart

*Not all wounds can
be easily healed.*

Once it had been firmly established that there were no snacks, the conference broke up quite quickly. The daytime creatures didn't like being out after dark, the night crew had food to look for and things to do, and many of them found being near their usual predators (or prey) extremely uncomfy – despite the unspoken truce that held sway at such rare communal events.

After the conference-goers had melted away into the cold October night, their way lit by a bright, waxing moon, only one remained among the tangled grass and seed heads of the wildflower area – the black-clad figure. Slowly, a silence fell.

'Thought you'd have a little meeting, did you?' the figure said, eventually.

Nobody replied.

'Too much to ask of you to invite one of your own kind, I suppose?'

'Oh, I'm – we're terribly sorry . . .' began Moss.

'I don't care about being left out, Moss, I'm used to it. I just came to tell you that what you're doing is pointless.'

'How do you know my name?' asked Moss, but just then Burnet stepped forward and spoke:

'Who are you?'

'And you're Burnet, and you both used to live in the last ash to survive from that nice little hedgerow. And Cumulus joined you, and you all had a lovely time, and now you don't have a home and your old friend's probably dead, and you're all very sad but you think you can save the world and make everything all right again. Well, you can't.'

Dormer put an arm around Moss, who had started to tremble.

'Oi,' began Spangle, puffing his feathers out belligerently – but Burnet laid an invisible, restraining hand on his wing.

'What's your name? I feel like I know you.'

'Mistle – and you do. Or, at the very least, you should.'

'Mistle . . .' Burnet said, clearly trying to remember. 'When . . .?'

'Ooh, five or six hundred cuckoo summers ago? But we've been neighbours for the last hundred – you've just been ignoring me.'

'I haven't, I swear!' said Burnet. 'I'm trying to think . . . did you used to look after a really old tree – I mean *really* old, like thousands and thousands of cuckoo summers? Have I got that right?'

Mistle's face was suddenly pinched with pain. 'A yew tree, the very oldest. An ancient, living being, a true witness to the world.'

'Oh no, I'm so sorry,' Moss said sympathetically. 'I expect Mortals cut it down, didn't they? Oh, we know *exactly* how you feel.'

'No, you don't!' snarled Mistle, whipping around to glare at Moss. 'None of you! You've got *absolutely no idea.*'

The confrontation felt frightening, because Mistle was so angry. But they could all see that the anger came from pain and sadness – and, moreover, it was clear that something important had brought the stranger here, something that hadn't yet been said. Moss took a step back and held Dormer's hand again, and everyone waited to see what would happen next.

'My yew tree was on a hillside not far from your patch, Burnet – the lime-tree wood. I remember it being felled, and you leaving, but I stayed on for a long time. The yew was so old it made even the most ancient oaks seem like babies, and it carried priceless wisdom and knowledge from the Old Time written deep into its heartwood. I didn't think that the changes going on in the Wild World would affect me. But then – then . . .'

Great heaving sobs began to wrack Mistle's black-clad body, but none of them dared approach to offer comfort.

'I'd been out foraging, and while I was away, two of our kind found it, and they – they moved in – just like that! They'd lost their special places and were wandering lost in the world, as so many were, and they – they wouldn't let me back in! They drove me away, they pelted me with stones, they said it was – it was *their* tree now . . .'

Mistle sunk to the ground, face in both hands, and wailed as though the terrible event had happened only yesterday – which is how it can feel, if you never talk about something that makes you really sad. If it isn't spoken out loud and listened to kindly, the feeling never has a chance to become bearable. It stays fresh.

As Mistle sobbed, Moss, Burnet and the others stared at one other, horrified. The idea that members of the Hidden Folk could simply take another's special place was sickening, and went against everything they knew about their own people. It was almost beyond belief.

'And that's not the worst of it,' managed Mistle, after a few moments. 'The worst of it is . . . they lit a fire, and – and . . .'

'The yew burnt down,' Burnet whispered. 'May Pan forgive them. I'm so sorry, Mistle. I didn't know.'

Mistle stood up again, and managed a deep, shaky breath. 'Anyway, that's not what I came here to tell you. I came to tell you to remember Robin Goodfellow's song – you know, the one about "Ash, oak and thorn"?'

'*Ash, oak and thorn were at the world's dawn . . .*' began Moss.

'*Rowan and yew will make it anew,*' finished Mistle. 'Except it can't, now, because it's gone – my yew tree, I mean. So there's no point to what you're doing. No point at all.'

Spangle made his excuses and went to roost in a bush, but the others kept Mistle talking for a while amid the grass stems, the moonlight picking out the shine on the newcomer's neatly sewn outfit, made from black bin bags. Without discussing it, they all felt that it was important to show kindness and try to prove that most Hidden Folk were safe to be friends with after all.

But Mistle clearly didn't much like or trust them, which was understandable, and every so often would say, 'I'm leaving now,' to which Moss would reply, 'Not yet!' or Sorrel would ask another question. Burnet, in particular, wanted to prove they hadn't been ignoring Mistle, who, it turned out, had lived in the school at the end of Ash Row since it was first built.

'I'm struggling to believe you didn't know I was there, to be honest,' Mistle said, with folded arms. 'I mean, *I* knew *you* were nearby – I think one of the Garden People first mentioned it, and, anyway, I sometimes saw the three of you in your garden when I was out exploring. It seemed obvious to me that you didn't want to be friends. You certainly never came over my way.'

'The thing is,' said Burnet, 'we'd got a bit . . . stuck in a rut, you know? We didn't leave the garden for ever such a long time – or the sheep field, before that. Honestly, we would have loved to know we had a neighbour, wouldn't we, Moss?'

'Oh yes!' said Moss. 'One of the reasons we went on our journey was to find more of our kind. And to think you were here all along!'

Dormer spoke up. 'Can I ask . . . I hope this doesn't seem rude, but are you, in actual fact, a Hob?'

'Oh, you go in for all that nonsense, do you?' asked Mistle, bluntly. Dormer looked a bit taken aback.

'Nonsense?'

'About there being different kinds of Hidden Folk. It's rubbish – haven't you worked that out yet? We're all the same, whether we live indoors or out. Doesn't matter what names you give us – Hobs or Hidden Folk, or even gnomes, if you must. We're all the same, and we should look out for one another. Not that it always works that way, but still.'

'Oh!' said Dormer.

'I have a question too,' said Sorrel. 'I've noticed you don't seem surprised at me and Burnet being partly invisible. I hope you don't mind me asking, but . . . are you fading too?'

Mistle's jacket fastened at the front with three toggles made from dandelion seeds. Once unbuttoned, they saw that, instead of a chest, there was nothing there at all – they could see right through to the back of the jacket.

'It started around my heart, and slowly got bigger. At one point I'd nearly disappeared – only my face, fingers and toes were left. But then I started to come back.'

'Come back? Really?' gasped Moss.

'What? How come?' said Burnet.

'Yes, it was ever so peculiar. Obviously I was relieved – when there was hardly any of me left, I started to feel . . . not tired, so much, but as though I wasn't really here. I just wish *all* of me had come back, though. I hate not being complete, I *hate* it.'

'But this changes *everything*!' said Sorrel excitedly. 'Let's try and work out what caused it to happen – because there must be a reason you came back, even partially. What happened around the time you started to become visible again?'

'Well, let me think . . . it wasn't long after I moved into the place where all the Mortal children go in the daytime. Not straight away, but around that time.'

'Interesting. And did you happen to eat any strange new foods, or drink any mysterious potions . . .?'

'I doubt it. I don't like new tastes.'

'Well, if nothing else, it's proof that the fading

can be reversed, even if we don't know how – and that's absolutely incredible!' said Sorrel. 'Mistle, you say there's no point to the efforts we're making, but I disagree. This is huge. This gives us hope.'

Dormer, who had been sitting quietly and listening, spoke up again.

'That song – you know, the one about ash, oak and thorn, and rowan and yew. That was made up by Robin Goodfellow, wasn't it?'

'Oh yes,' said Mistle. 'A very long time ago.'

'I remember old Dodder singing it, you know,' said Burnet. 'The Folly Oak was very ancient. Not as old as your yew, of course, but still special.'

'The song is more than an old rhyme,' continued Mistle. 'It's a prophecy. A clue to how the world could have been remade, with the help of a rowan and a yew – *my* yew, obviously, as the oldest. But it's gone.'

'I bet there are rowans in this area,' said Dormer, thoughtfully. 'They're good trees for a Hive: not too big, and with pretty berries in autumn. Whether or not Mortals know about their special powers, they definitely like having them around.'

'And I bet I can find a yew somewhere, too,' said Burnet. 'What do you reckon, everyone? If Mistle's right, and the song is a clue left by Robin

Goodfellow, we should at least try to find the magical trees – and who knows what might happen next?'

In a cosy nest box fixed to the fence of a lovely tangly garden on a street called Ash Row, Moss lay awake in the dark. Snores issued from the neighbouring box, and the others were silent. It was the hour before dawn, and outside the second frost of the year was painting the sleeping garden silver.

Despite Mistle's astonishing news that the fading could be reversed, Moss felt uncomfortable with how fast things were moving. All of a sudden, Burnet was talking about going off on a quest to find some trees, just because they were mentioned in an old rhyme! Of course, as someone who loved stories and legends, Moss was never going to laugh at them or think they were silly – but it just didn't feel like the right thing to be doing.

'It won't take long, I promise,' Burnet had said. 'And it won't hold anything up – you can still get on with your plan of talking to Ro and helping the Wild World, can't you? You don't need me for that bit anyway.'

But then, after talking more to Mistle, Burnet had decided to enlist Spangle – 'He can fly, Moss, and, anyway, he's not on board with the whole Mortals plan' – and even asked Dormer for help looking for the kinds of places where Mortals might have planted rowan trees! Moss had looked at Dormer, stricken, but Dormer had smiled reassuringly, saying, 'I think you can manage without me, Burnet. I'm going to stick with Moss.' And then, of course, Sorrel had decided to go off alone and invent a new house, so the sparrow tribe could have their special boxes back. It all felt oddly painful, as though, having made it all the way home again, their little gang was somehow breaking up.

But you can't force your friends to do what you want them to do, and sometimes there are lots of different ways to try and achieve the same goal. In the morning Ro would come and find them again, and Moss would ask for her help. Maybe she could work out how to make next-door's garden more welcoming for wildlife. She could talk to the children who lived there, and they'd start feeding the birds, or making a pond, and that would be the start of their new job of saving the Wild World, one garden at a time. How hard could it be?

16
How to disappear

Could Moss and Dormer
be becoming invisible?

First thing the next morning, they all rappelled down into the garden, where Moss made everyone a delicious breakfast of warm hazelnut porridge topped with a tiny, glossy segment of blackberry each. When Spangle arrived, Burnet brought him up to date with the previous night's discussions, and he agreed to help with the search for a rowan and a yew tree in the local streets and parks.

Not long after the two of them had headed off, deep in discussion about particular roads and the direction the sun came from, Sorrel left to explore the garden and scope out the best spot to build an ultra-modern home, saying, 'I may be an excellent inventor, but still, location is *everything*, you know.'

That left Moss and Dormer to wait for Ro to come and see them, as she'd promised she would.

146

'Will she find us down here, do you think?' asked Dormer, once they had put out their little cooking fire safely, and washed the tin cauldron with melted frost.

'Any moment now she'll come and look in the nest boxes, and then we can call out to her,' said Moss.

'Or I could play my flute.'

'Or you could play your flute.'

They waited . . . and waited . . . and waited. Spink the chaffinch came to say hello, and then bustled away again. A straggling skein of pink-footed geese flew over slowly, small and high in the dawn sky. The last of the leaves fell from the trees and drifted down. And as the sun rose, the frost slowly melted where the light touched it, but remained silvery-white in the shade.

'Maybe she's forgotten,' said Dormer, after a while. 'Or . . . maybe she stayed over at her auntie's last night.'

'She'll be here,' said Moss. 'I trust her. Don't forget, Mortals get up far, far later than Animalkind.'

Just then they heard the back door open and close again, and the thunderous sound of running feet.

147

'Over here!' called Moss, standing up and waving both arms, as Dormer blew an unexpectedly loud and slightly alarming *parp* on the little white plastic pipe. It felt very strange to be deliberately trying to attract the attention of a Mortal, and their hearts were pounding as two huge feet in trainers made straight for them, a pair of denim-clad knees descended to ground level, and a happy brown face with curly hair appeared above them.

'Hello, tiny people!'

'Hello, Mortal child!' replied Moss and Dormer, at exactly the same time. And then they all just smiled at each other, for quite a long moment. It felt surprisingly nice to all three of them, and it was a moment that none of them would ever forget.

'Were you warm enough in the bird boxes?' asked Ro. 'Looks like it was a pretty frosty night.'

'Yes, thank you – though we're going to move out soon, and let the sparrows have them back,' replied Moss. 'Sorrel's going to invent us a house somewhere in your garden. Do you mind?'

'That'd be brilliant! Where?'

'We're not sure yet, but we'll let you know.'

'And what's Burnet up to?'

'Gone to look for trees, along with Spangle – our starling friend.'

'Yes, Mistle told them where to look,' added Dormer.

'Who's that, a thrush?'

'Oh no, Mistle's one of us,' Dormer replied.

'Mistle lives in that place all you Mortal children go,' explained Moss. 'You know, the big building at the top of the road.'

'St Swithin's? Oh, that's my school. You probably don't have them. It's like . . . a place where you go to learn things.'

'Wow, that sounds *amazing*!' said Moss.

'S'all right,' said Ro. 'It's pretty cool that one of you lives there, though. I never knew that. Can you tell Mistle I want to be friends?'

'Erm . . .' said Moss, doubtfully.

'We can try . . .' said Dormer.

'Anyway, there's no school all week 'cos of half-term. What shall we play?'

'Do you know Acorn Hop?' asked Dormer, hopefully. It would be fun to play with someone even newer to the game, and moreover, Burnet had recently passed on some slightly unorthodox techniques.

But Moss nudged Dormer hard in the ribs. 'We're not here to play games – sorry, both of you. Don't you remember, Dormer? We have some very important business to discuss with Mortalkind.'

'Oh!' said Ro, putting on her most serious face. 'OK, I'm ready. Go.'

So Moss told her everything that had happened since they had lost their ash-tree home in next-door's garden: how they had travelled to the countryside in search of their cousins, and had met Sorrel instead; how they had then journeyed deep into the heart of the Hive – 'That's where I came into it,' said Dormer – and what they had learnt there about the fate of the Hidden Folk; and finally what Cumulus had said about finding a new job in the Wild World, so that they wouldn't all fade away.

'And that's why you've come back?' asked Ro at the end of it.

'Yes,' said Moss, firmly. 'And we need your help. The plan is to make next-door's garden like this one – you know, with more of the types of plants that insects need, and maybe some bird feeders, and make all of it less—'

'Tidy and boring,' said Ro. 'I know exactly what you mean.'

'And we thought, seeing as you're friends with the children who live there, you could—'

'Wait – did I say that?'

'I think so,' said Moss. 'Didn't she, Dormer?'

'I can't remember,' said Dormer, truthfully.

'We're not *friends*-friends. I mean, we're not *not* friends, if you see what I mean, but Maya's two years older than me, and Ben's a year younger. We go to the same school, but we don't play together or anything. I don't really know them all that well.'

'Oh,' said Moss, sounding crestfallen.

'Can you make friends with them?' asked Dormer.

'I can try, it's just that . . . I'm not sure if either of them is very interested in nature. I mean, I know Maya collects stuffed animals, but—'

'She collects *what*?' said Moss.

'Oh – just toys. Stuffed animal toys. And I think Ben watches nature programmes on telly, but that's not the same as liking it in real life.'

'What's telly?' asked Dormer.

'Too hard to explain. Anyway, what I'm saying is that, even if I did make friends with them, I don't think they'd really care about what lives in their garden. It's just not that interesting to them.'

Moss and Dormer looked at one another, confused. How could anyone not be interested in the Wild World they were part of, with all its secrets and dramas and tragedies and excitements?

What in the name of Pan could be more fascinating than that?

'I know – I don't get it either,' said Ro. '"Horses for courses," Dad says, but I don't understand what horses have got to do with anything. My dad says some really weird things sometimes.'

'Look,' said Moss. 'Failure is not an option. We have to find a way to make next-door's garden as good as this one. It's the only way to save Cumulus, and all the rest of our kind. How can we *make* them care about the Wild World?'

'I don't think we can,' said Ro, doubtfully. 'You can't force people to like things. It doesn't work.'

'All right. How can we *entice* them to make the garden better?' said Moss. 'How about you make them feel really, really bad and guilty about not looking after nature more!'

'I think that's a *terrible* idea. Nobody likes to feel bad!'

'I know: what if it was a competition?' suggested Dormer. 'Like, who's got the most wild creatures living in their garden? Would they want to do it then?'

'I reckon there's only one thing for it,' said Ro. 'You'll have to show yourselves. It's the only way to get them interested.'

An hour or so later, Moss and Dormer were sitting under the evergreen shrub in Moss's old garden, waiting for Maya to come out of the house. Bravely, Ro had agreed to knock on the door and ask if she wanted to play. The plan was for the two girls to go out into the garden, at which point Dormer and Moss would stroll past and let themselves be seen. Then they'd tell Maya all about the Garden People, and hopefully she'd be so amazed by everything that she'd want to do all she could to help.

But it had been ages now, and the back door remained firmly closed. Ro had warned them it might be tricky to get Maya to go outdoors, especially on a cold day, and Moss started to worry that they were just going to play inside.

At last there came the squeak of the door opening and Mr B the blackbird let out his loud, clucking alarm call. It was a sound that had once been so familiar – a signal to scurry back into their ash-tree home. This time, though, Moss simply gave Dormer's hand a squeeze.

'Ready, Dormer?' And Dormer nodded, bravely.

As the two girls walked towards them across the

lawn, they could hear the unintelligible, booming sound of their Mortal language, so different from the Wild Argot Ro spoke so naturally with them. Moss peeked out and saw a taller girl with Ro; her hair was in a ponytail, and she wore a pink coat. When the two pairs of feet were drawing close to the evergreen bush, Moss and Dormer gathered all their courage – and strolled out on to the grass.

They had expected some kind of surprised kerfuffle, or even a scream, perhaps. But what actually happened was . . . nothing. Ro's trainers stopped as she saw them and waited for Maya to notice, but Maya's trainers just carried on walking by. Looking up, Moss could see Ro's face high above them, looking incredibly confused; after a moment's pause, she ran to catch up with the older girl.

'Wait, what just happened?' asked Dormer. 'Were we in the wrong place, or was she looking the other way?'

'I'm not sure,' said Moss. 'Let's try again. Come on, there's a trail that runs through this flower bed. We can cut through and intercept them down by the back fence.'

At the end of the garden they tried again, walking out directly in front of the two girls. Once again, Ro saw them, and looked back and forth between Maya and the place where they stood. But Maya just didn't seem to register anything unusual. At last, growing frustrated, Moss ran out and jumped up and down in front of her, waving both arms and shouting. She was looking in exactly the right direction, but seemed to see nothing at all.

As the two Mortal children walked back towards the house, Ro looked over to where Moss and Dormer stood on the lawn and gave a very puzzled shrug.

Moss and Dormer were back under the evergreen shrub, tucking into some acorn bread sandwiches with hawthorn pickle and mushroom that Moss had packed for their lunch.

'I just don't get it,' Dormer said. 'Ro can see us. Why not Maya?'

'I don't know. I just wish Cumulus was here to ask,' said Moss, with a sigh. 'You know, spending time in this garden again really takes me back to the old days when we were all together. It makes me feel sad.'

'I can understand that,' said Dormer. 'When you love someone, and you really miss them, it can be hard to be reminded of them.'

The back door opened, but Mr B was elsewhere and neither Moss nor Dormer heard it.

'I just feel so hopeless,' continued Moss. 'How are we going to prove to Pan we're still useful if we can't enlist the help of Mortals? Maybe it was a stupid idea all along – after all, it's all only guess-work. We don't know for sure what we're supposed to do to make the world better, or how to fulfil Robin Goodfellow's prophecy. We've probably got it all wrong.'

'Come on, let's climb back over the fence, get into our nest boxes and wait for the others to come back,' said Dormer, standing up and offering Moss a hand. 'Then we can talk it all through properly – together. What do you think?'

But just as they emerged from under the shrub, a huge football whizzed over their heads and crashed into the flower bed behind them. They both ducked and tried to scurry back under cover – and as they did so, they heard a voice.

It was Maya's brother, the little boy Moss had shared a garden with for eight whole cuckoo summers: first as a tiny baby carried by his parents, then as a chubby toddler, staggering around and putting snails and bits of grass in his mouth, then a child who loved bouncing on the trampoline and kicking a ball around. He had never shown any curiosity about things like the interesting-looking hole at the bottom of the ash tree's trunk, or the first blackbird song of spring, and he'd certainly never noticed the three Hidden Folk he shared his garden with – until now.

'Wow,' said Ben, looking down at the two of them now. 'What on *earth* are you?'

17

And so it begins . . .

Ben the Mortal boy
is let into a very big secret.

'. . . and he said to come back tomorrow and he'd tell us what happened!' concluded Dormer, breathlessly. It was getting on for evening and the Hidden Folk were gathered in Ro's shrubbery to eat their dinner around a little campfire and discuss the day's events.

'Wait,' said Burnet, who seemed in a slightly cross mood but wouldn't admit it. 'So this boy, this . . . *Ben*. He could see you, but his sister couldn't?'

'Yep,' said Moss and Dormer, together.

'What do you think about this, Mistle? You see a lot of Mortal children at your "school" place, or whatever it's called. Can some of them see you, and some of them not?'

'No idea,' said Mistle shortly. It was the first thing their guest had said all evening.

Spangle had flown over to the school with an invitation from Moss to come to dinner, and Mistle had immediately said no. The problem with hurt and loneliness is that they can make people avoid the one thing that might help them feel better – spending time with others – in case it goes wrong and they get hurt again. Despite using all his charm, Spangle had left the school playground with no idea whether Mistle would turn up or not, so everyone felt pleased when their reluctant guest arrived.

'Anyway,' said Moss, 'we plan to go back tomorrow and talk to the Mortal boy again, and see if he's spoken to the grown-ups and whether they've agreed to any of our ideas.'

'Which were what, exactly?' said Burnet.

'Well, we haven't had a chance to speak to the Garden People yet and find out all their requests, but we thought we'd start with a mini pond, a wildflower patch and a bird feeder, and sort of . . . take it from there.'

Burnet didn't say anything, just threw another twig on to the fire, moodily.

'Well, I think that all sounds brilliant,' said Sorrel. 'Well done, you two. Would anyone like to hear how my day went?'

159

'Yes, please,' said Moss, who was starting to wonder if Burnet might have had had a difficult day looking for trees.

'So,' began Sorrel. 'At first I was thinking of building us a tree house, and I spent the morning climbing all the suitable trees and looking for a good spot. A tree house needs a stable platform: high enough off the ground to be safe from cats, but not so high that it might wobble in the wind. And you want a view, but without being too visible – anyway, the upshot is, I couldn't find anywhere quite right.'

'Can't we just stay in our boxes?' asked Burnet.

'It's not really fair on the sparrows,' said Sorrel. 'Anyway, I've had a brilliant idea. I'm going to build us . . . an underground house!'

There was a long moment of silence.

'Like a . . . burrow?' said Dormer, who'd never quite got over being lost in the badger sett. 'Won't it be dark?'

'Nope – there'll be windows. Overhead ones – you'll see.'

'Sounds damp,' said Burnet. 'I hate the damp. Gets in my bones.'

'It won't be damp either, I promise. Trust me, I'm an inventor.'

'How long will it take to build?' asked Moss. 'Seeing as we're not going to sleep through winter, it would be nice to have a really cosy home – one all four of us can be in together.'

'Sounds nice for you,' said Mistle.

'Oh! I meant for you too!' said Moss, quickly. 'Sorrel, there'll be room for Mistle, won't there?'

'Don't worry, I wasn't being serious,' replied Mistle, curtly. 'I don't want to live with you anyway.'

'Erm . . . and how was your day, Burnet?' asked Dormer, to smooth over Moss's obvious embarrassment. 'Did you and Spangle find a rowan and a yew?'

'Almost – Spangle spotted two whitebeams that had been planted by the side of a death-chariot route, and they're the same family as rowans. But no rowan yet, and certainly no yew,' said Burnet.

'Where is Spangle, by the way?' asked Dormer.

'He said something about roosting with some chaffinches,' said Burnet. 'I think he might be missing his own kind, you know. He was talking about murmurations again today.'

'What's a murmuration?' asked Moss.

'When hundreds and hundreds of starlings get together in winter and perform a sort of sky ballet

161

just before bedtime,' explained Dormer. 'They used to do it in the Hive until about fifty cuckoo summers ago.'

'I wonder if they do it at that winter conference he goes to,' mused Moss. 'In fact, isn't it about time for him to fly to the east coast?'

'I mentioned that to him today, but he said he'd stick around and help us,' said Burnet. 'He's such a good friend, isn't he? We should make sure we give him lots of love this winter. Some birds are solitary, but not starlings. We mustn't forget that.'

'I'm going now,' said Mistle, getting up and walking away into the darkness. 'Thanks for dinner or whatever – it wasn't disgusting. Before I go: you were asking about Mortal children. Well, some are better at noticing than others. There's a blackbird where I live called Turdus – distant cousin of your friend Bob, I believe. And you know how in spring all the males add a different flourish to the end of their songs? Well, *his* flourish sounds like the noise that comes out of those black boxes Mortals love so much. Some of the children have noticed this, and they seem to like it, so they recognize Turdus and take an interest in how he's doing. But lots of them don't see him at all, like he's not even there in the playground, let alone making a beeping sound. So, for what it's worth, I'd guess that being able to see our kind is exactly the same thing.'

'Turdus is a funny name,' said Moss, struggling to suppress a giggle.

'I named him that!' replied Mistle irritably. 'And it's perfect for him, I'll have you know.'

And with that, their guest was gone.

The next morning was one of the best Moss had had since they had set out from the Hive. The sadness and grief about Cumulus was still there, as it was for all of them, but finally making progress and doing something worthwhile felt good. And it was exciting to wake up and know they were going to speak to more actual Mortals – whoever would have thought they could actually communicate properly, like other animals! It was an amazing discovery.

After they'd all had breakfast, and Sorrel and Burnet had gone off to get on with their separate missions, Moss and Dormer climbed over the fence to next-door's garden and did a tour of all the Garden People they could find there: the parakeets and squirrels, the blackbirds and dunnocks, the earthworms and earwigs and grey house mice. By the time the Mortals in the house were having breakfast, Moss and Dormer had put together a long list of requests and demands. Many were contradictory, as they'd expected, but what they both knew (and would never have said out loud) was that for a place to work properly, some of the inhabitants need to eat some of the other inhabitants, and that's just the way it is. The secret, they remembered from their time as guardians, was for everything to be in balance, so that there were lots and lots of the very small, very important things, which helped ensure there were good numbers of whatever ate them, and enough of whatever ate *them*, all the way to the creatures at the top of the pyramid, like the sparrowhawks, who could be few and far between.

It wasn't long until Ben came out of the house in a red bobble hat and gloves, trailing a threadbare blue bunny by one grubby ear. Dormer blew a *parp* on the little plastic flute to show the little boy where they were, and he ran over. He agreed to knock on Ro's door and invite her over to play, and before long all four of them were crouched under the trampoline, out of sight of any grown-ups who might be looking out of the house.

'I like your trampoline,' said Ro shyly.

'Thanks. It's my sister's really. You can go on it if you want.'

'Maybe later,' Ro replied. 'Can you believe that Hidden Folk are real, though, not just in books! And they lived in your garden this entire time!'

Ben grinned. 'I know! It's better than a puppy. Puppies are cute at first, but not for ever, and these are for ever.'

'But now they live in *my* garden, 'cos it's better, so I can play with them whenever I want,' said Ro.

Moss felt it was important to interrupt this conversation. 'Excuse me! We're not pets!'

'Or toys,' said Dormer.

'You're animals,' said Ben, uncertainly.

'Not exactly.'

'You're *nature*,' said Ro, confidently.

'We are. Just like you.'

Ben and Ro stared at each other. 'Us?' said Ro. 'But we're not nature!'

'Yes, you are,' said Dormer, firmly. 'You're alive, aren't you?'

'Well . . . yeah. But nature's . . . natural.'

'And *you're* natural, too. You just forgot.'

'I didn't,' said Ben, letting out a big burp and collapsing into giggles. 'I'm natural!' he shouted, taking his gloves off and rubbing his hands on the damp winter lawn. Then he rubbed some mud on to his cheeks and pulled a silly face.

'Ben, you have to be *serious*,' said Ro, sternly. 'Moss and Dormer need our help, and their friends do too. We're the only ones who can save the Hidden Folk.'

'And the entire Wild World, too,' said Moss.

Ben stopped being silly and looked as though he might be about to cry. 'I don't want to have to save things – it's scary and hard,' he said, in a small voice.

'I told you, he's only a kid,' said Ro, rolling her eyes as though she was a decade older than Ben instead of one year, two months and eleven days.

'Hey, Ben, do you remember what we talked about yesterday?' asked Dormer. 'About feeding the birds?'

'Yeah,' said Ben, sniffing a little.

'And what did the grown-ups say when you asked them?'

'They said I could use my pocket money.'

'What's "money"?' Moss asked, turning to Ro.

'Too hard to explain. So, Ben,' Ro continued, 'when are you going to the shops?'

'Mum said after lunch.'

'Can I come? I can show you the best kind of bird seed to get and everything.'

'OK,' said Ben. 'Maya's coming too, though. She's getting colouring pencils.'

'That's all right,' said Ro, grinning. 'I like colouring too.'

For the rest of the morning the four of them explored the garden. To any grown-ups looking out of the kitchen window – or to Maya, for that matter – it would just have looked like Ben and Ro were playing with small things on the ground: sticks, perhaps, or acorns, or leaves. But what was really happening was that Moss was showing the two children, and Dormer, all the garden's secrets: the tiny, winding passageways that led through the flower beds and were used by everything from Hidden Folk to shrews; the safe place under the laurel bush; a cache of nuts and seeds left by a wood mouse; the entrance hole to an underground chamber where a furry queen bumblebee was hibernating; and a tiny, empty wren's nest, left over from spring. Everywhere they went, Moss explained which of the Garden People had made what and how they lived, and Ro talked to Ben about what kind of things they might be able to do to help. To the two Hidden Folk, it felt strange but exciting to be sharing their secret world with two curious children, and they both hoped it might be the start of something wonderful.

Which made what happened next even more extraordinary. Because when Ben and Ro had gone back indoors for their lunch, and Moss and Dormer had scrambled back over the fence, they saw Burnet's excited face poking out from his nest box.

'Oh, hello!' called out Moss. 'You're back early!'

'I know, I rushed straight back!' said Burnet, tossing out a neatly tied rope, ready to climb down. 'Not only did we find the most *amazing* rowan tree, but look!' And here their dear friend waved two completely visible arms out of the nest-box hole, complete with hands. 'Isn't it incredible? Both of my arms have come back!'

18

Grand designs

*Sorrel completes work
on their new home.*

The days that followed seemed to pass in a complete blur. The fact that not only Mistle but now Burnet had somehow reversed the fading process – even if only partially – spurred everyone into a whirlwind of hopeful activity.

Moss and Dormer spent every waking hour in the garden of 52 Ash Row, thinking of ways to make it more nature-friendly. Ben had bought a little bird feeder with his pocket money, and they consulted with Spuggie and Spink about the best place to hang it, and extracted a promise from Carlos not to guzzle all the seed without leaving any for anyone else. They helped Ben and Ro to make a cosy hedgehog home from sticks and leaves, just in case one should ever find its way under the side gate looking for shelter, and, when it got too cold to

169

play outside for long, the two children sat indoors and began making plans and drawings for a pond.

Meanwhile, Burnet and Spangle were redoubling their efforts to find a yew tree. Burnet was convinced that the discovery of the rowan had reversed the fading and was the first step to fulfilling Robin Goodfellow's prophecy; if they found a yew, Burnet believed it might bring Sorrel's left arm and leg back, or even make Cumulus appear again somewhere in the Wild World. Tirelessly they scoured the streets, gardens, parks and every scrap of wood they could find, Spangle flying overhead and the stalwart Burnet ending each day exhausted and covered in scratches and bruises from climbing over and under fences and battling through deep drifts of leaves.

Moss wasn't convinced by their plan, and neither was Dormer, but they had to admit that Burnet's arms had reappeared the exact same day the rowan tree was discovered – a day when they hadn't yet made any progress on the garden. Moreover, since then, they'd done loads of good things next door, yet no other part of them had reappeared: not Burnet's legs, nor Sorrel's left side, nor Mistle's missing heart. Moss tried to hold on to the belief that what they were doing was helpful and good, and the best way to create a new job for themselves in the world, but it wasn't always easy to stay positive. Still, there was nothing for it but to keep working, keep trying, and keep hoping that they were on the right track.

The nights got colder, and darkness fell a little earlier each day. Each evening the Hidden Folk and Spangle gathered in the shrubbery under the nest boxes to discuss the day's events. Although they were all doing different things in the daytime, it was important to come together and talk things through over dinner; it helped them all feel like a team. Sometimes Mistle, who was slowly becoming less prickly, joined them, and even smiled once or twice. But their new friend rarely stayed for dinner, and would always go back to the darkened school at the end of the road to sleep.

The fact that there were only four nest boxes seemed to underline the fact that Mistle wasn't fully part of the group, despite their best intentions. Sorrel, in particular, felt it keenly, and worked flat out on building a home with space for all of them – even though Mistle showed no sign of ever wanting to live with them there. Now and again the others offered to help, but there was nothing Sorrel loved more than working alone and solving problems singlehandedly – with a little bit of help from the Garden People every now and then.

At last the day came when their new home was finally ready. Before they ate their dinner, while there was still a little light left in the sky, Sorrel led them through the undergrowth towards the end of the garden.

Spangle came too – just out of curiosity, he assured them.

'Won't ever catch me underground again, no way,' he muttered, bringing up the rear of the little procession. 'Just need to know where you lot are at, so's I can keep an eye on you.'

They came to a spot near the log pile where Cora the frog was currently hibernating.

'Watch carefully,' whispered Sorrel, and pressed the end of one of the smaller pieces of wood. Soundlessly, it swung inward, revealing a secret passageway. Sorrel stepped inside – and disappeared.

With a mixture of excitement and trepidation, the others followed – all except Spangle, who stayed by the log pile muttering quietly to himself. Inside, light filtered in from between the cleverly placed sticks and branches above, illuminating a set of steps that took them down, into the ground.

The steps led to a short passageway, at the end of which they found a comfortable chamber with a floor of beaten earth, a round table made from a section of log, and walls where Sorrel had started to fit a few little cabinets. Best of all, plenty of light shone in from above, where a clear, convex window had been installed.

'Isn't it brilliant?' Sorrel said, proudly. 'Ro got it for me out of the bin, and we cleaned it together – Mortal food came in it, apparently. If we ever need to disguise it, we can sprinkle some earth over it, though I don't think we will. Oh, and I'm hoping Moss will weave us a lovely grass mat for the floor, and over time we can line the walls with cupboards, can't we? Anyway, let me show you all to your rooms!'

Five little sleeping chambers led off the central chamber, just big enough for each of them to curl up in their sleeping bags. There was an escape tunnel, too. 'I got the idea from the badger sett,' said Sorrel, standing proudly at the tunnel entrance. 'It comes out at the edge of the wild-flower patch, under a big clump of comfrey.'

Burnet gazed around smiling, newly visible arms folded. 'What an amazing job you've done, Sorrel!

It's not dark or damp at all – in fact, it's cosy and welcoming. Thank you, dear friend. You've invented us the most incredible home.'

'Yes, thank you, Sorrel!' said Moss, going over for a hug. 'I love it – and of *course* I'll make us a rug. The best one ever.'

'I can't believe it!' said Dormer. 'I mean, you made us a boat in no time at all, and the others have told me about "Thunderbolt", your trusty chariot. But this – this is something else.'

Sorrel blushed. 'I hope we'll be happy here for as long as we're all – well, for as long as possible. And I really hope Mistle comes to join us one day, too.'

'Oi,' came a voice from above. 'Are you lot ever coming out? Some of us need to go and roost for the night!'

'Sorry, Spangle!' they called, and trooped dutifully back up the steps, where Sorrel showed them how to work the secret mechanism that opened the little wooden door in the log pile.

'Shall we have one last night in the bird boxes?' asked Moss, once they were back out in the open air.

'Oh no,' said Burnet. 'The thing you have to realize, Moss, is that it's not fair on the sparrows. I vote that after dinner we move in straight away!'

Before long, the four Hidden Folk felt as though they had lived under the woodpile for many a cuckoo summer, rather than for six days and nights. Moss wove the most beautiful round rug from dry meadow grasses and wildflower stems, Burnet consulted with Sorrel about the prevailing wind and together they built a chimney and set a little fireplace into one wall of the main chamber. Meanwhile, Dormer got the two children to bring them empty boxes and bits of packaging and set about making cupboards like the ones Mac and Min had had back in the Hive.

After breakfast each morning, Burnet, and sometimes Sorrel, would set out to meet Spangle and continue the search for a yew. More often, though, Sorrel accompanied Moss and Dormer next door, where the three of them worked hard to transform the dormant garden, ready for spring. They searched for butterfly, ladybird and grasshopper eggs and made sure they were safe from frost by packing them with fluffy clematis seed heads if they looked too exposed to the cold winter air. Then they scoured every flower bed for stray seeds, setting aside the ones the Garden People most needed so that they could be properly planted and watered and have the best chance come spring. Sometimes Ben and Ro helped, though the light was usually fading by the time they'd got back from school and done their homework. And once or twice Maya came into the garden, but she still couldn't see them – even when they passed really close by.

It was well past the time when Hidden Folk usually begin their long winter sleep, and Moss had expected to start feeling tired – but it didn't happen, perhaps because they all had such a sense of purpose in their lives. And what's more, it was interesting to watch as the final few chiffchaffs flew south, the wasps, comma butterflies and bats hibernated, and the trees lost their last leaves, so that their bare branches stood out black against the winter sky. To witness the ivy's November blossom and see fungi sprouting from the rich, damp earth was part of the year's natural cycle, which they had never been awake for before, and everything that went on was interesting to see.

They had been back at Ash Row for long enough to start to feel settled, when something happened that would change everything. The first hint of the change to come was that Ben and Maya's parents came out of the house and spent two whole days tidying the garden. They cut back all the dead plants and shrubs and made a big bonfire, after which everything smelt of smoke, and the flower beds looked very bare and bleak. They washed the decking with harsh chemicals, planted scentless, imported flowers in the big pots that stood on it, and got out the fancy garden furniture that had been stored away in the shed. Then some other grown-ups arrived and took photos, after which a big red-and-white sign went up by the gate at the front of the house.

And then, one Saturday morning, Ben came out to the garden, looking for them, and it seemed as though he'd been crying.

Dormer signalled to him with the flute, and the little boy came over to the cold ashes of the bonfire, where they were checking to see if any useful seeds or insect eggs had survived the terrible blaze.

'What's the matter, Ben?' asked Moss. 'Did you get told off at school?'

'Was your sister mean to you?' added Dormer, sympathetically. 'You know she loves you really, don't you? I bet she was only teasing.'

But Ben just shook his head and wiped his nose on the back of his glove.

'What is it, then?' asked Moss.

'Mummy and Daddy said – they said we're moving.'

'What do you mean? Moving where?'

'To live in a different house, because it's bigger. I don't know where, because I haven't seen it. I can still go to the same school, but . . . I won't be able to finish the garden, and I won't be able to play with you any more!'

'Oh, Ben, don't cry,' said Dormer. 'Just think how exciting it'll be to have a whole new house to get to know! And anyway, you can make the garden nice there, can't you?'

'Dormer's right,' said Moss. 'You can find out who lives there, and what they need – the great thing is, you know how to do that now!'

'But what about here? What about *this* garden?'

'We'll look after it – won't we, Dormer?'

'Absolutely. Of course we will.'

With their help, Ben quickly started to feel better, but Moss was left with a sinking feeling. Not only would they really miss the little boy, but it felt as though all the work they'd put into the garden was suddenly under threat.

19

Nothing left

*Moss and Burnet encounter
their greatest foe.*

'I'm not gonna lie, I'm concerned for the both of 'em,' said Spangle. It was a few days later, and he was talking to Sorrel inside the covered bird table in Ro's garden, where Spangle was pecking up the tasty dried mealworms Ro's dad had put out for his kind to eat.

'I'm worried too,' said Sorrel. 'Moss has hardly got out of bed for a whole week, and Burnet hasn't spoken in days. Do you think they're starting to miss their winter sleep? I feel all right myself.'

'It ain't that,' said Spangle. 'What it is, is they've run out.'

'Run out?'

'You saw how hard they were grafting to try and save the Wild World. And now it's gone wrong, they got no energy left.'

179

Sorrel sighed. 'Not a single yew tree in the entire area, and now the whole future of their old garden's at stake.'

It turned out that the bad news about next door was even worse than they'd first thought: as well as the house being sold, part of the garden was being turned into a car park for a new doctor's surgery that was due to be built nearby. The lawn and flower beds, the shed and the spot where the hollow ash tree had once stood would all disappear under tarmac. Only the wooden decking area near the back door would survive.

'All that work Moss and Dormer did on the garden – wasted,' said Spangle, shaking his sleek little head. 'Proper crying shame, that is.'

'How can we cheer them up?' asked Sorrel. 'I hate seeing them like this. Maybe I could invent something fun.'

'Not sure about that, Boss,' said Spangle. 'Sometimes you just gotta let people feel whatever they're feeling. Don't forget they're grieving for Cumulus now, n'all.'

'How'd you mean?'

'Well, as long as they were rushing around thinking they were going to reverse the fading, they didn't have to face up to their pal being gone for ever, you get me? Now they've both given up hope of that – *bam*. The sad feelings come.'

Sorrel sighed. 'You're right, Spangle. I just wish I could help them. Our new house is nearly finished, bar a few cabinets, and I . . . I don't know how to be useful any more.'

'*Be* with them,' said the wise little starling. 'Show 'em you care. And don't *you* give up, either – something'll come along and change everything. Just you wait and see.'

When they had first moved into the subterranean home under the log pile, Moss had thought it was cosy and welcoming, always full of chatter and excitement. Now, though, it was silent, and the air felt somehow stale. Thanks to the fireplace, the rooms were still warm, despite the weather outside being the coldest that Moss had ever experienced; but the Hidden Folk's sadness was affecting the way the whole dwelling felt.

When the news came that the garden was to be turned into a car park, Moss had felt both anger and disbelief. After it came sadness, and both Moss and Burnet had cried on and off for two whole days

– for Cumulus, and for the future they'd both imagined, which would now never come to pass. The hope that had been keeping them going seemed to have vanished, and with it, their energy, too. And knowing how much their friends were worrying about them made it all feel worse.

Moss was lying in bed, staring at the ceiling, when Sorrel got back from seeing Spangle and had a quiet conversation with Dormer at the foot of the steps. It was a conversation Moss accidentally overheard.

'Moss is asleep again, and Burnet keeps saying nothing's the matter, even though it is,' murmured Dormer, in a worried voice. 'I've suggested a story, or a game of Acorn Hop, but neither of them even replied. I even offered to play a lovely tune on my flute, but they're not interested in *anything*.'

'I've just seen Spangle, and he says we don't need to cheer them up,' replied Sorrel quietly. 'He said to just let them be sad, until it passes.'

'That's what I've been trying to do,' said Dormer, 'but it's hard – especially as they're both lost in their own little worlds, not even comforting each other. Moss doesn't even seem to care what we eat, which is *very* out of character. That never happened at Mac and Min's, not even after the cat bite.'

'Yes, that definitely isn't a good sign.'

'Anyway, Sorrel, I've been meaning to ask: how are *you*?'

'It's really kind of you to ask,' came Sorrel's reply. 'I suppose . . . well, I wasn't convinced that *either* of their plans would work, if I'm honest. But part of me hoped I was wrong – that my left arm and leg would magically reappear and I wouldn't fade away after all. I'm sure Burnet's feeling the same way too – maybe even worse than I am, having got both arms back. It doesn't seem fair.'

'I think we're all feeling it, to different degrees,' said Dormer. 'Still, I keep reminding myself that Robin Goodfellow wasn't at all frightened of vanishing, so I shouldn't be either.'

'And who knows: maybe we'll meet old Cumulus again in the next place,' said Sorrel, sadly. 'Now, I'm going to make lunch, and then shall we go and sit with the others for a bit?'

'I was just popping out for some fresh air, actually,' said Dormer. 'You lot have turned me from an indoor creature to an outdoor one – now I need to get out and see what the Wild World's up to every day!' And Moss heard the secret door in the logpile opening and closing as Dormer went out.

Sorrel brought a bit of lunch in and sat quietly

on the edge of Moss's bed, and after a while went away. Moss dozed, stared at the network of fine white rootlets in the earth wall, and now and again put some rhymes together ('Dormer/warmer', for example), or thought of a nice way of saying something, out of habit – but that was all. An occasional sigh could be heard from the main chamber, where Burnet was sitting cross-legged, gazing into the fire, every so often feeding it a fragment of pine cone, or poking it with a piece of wire.

Meanwhile, indoors at 52 Ash Row all the books and toys and clothes were being packed away into boxes, the rugs rolled up and the curtains taken down. Above the heads of all the busy Mortals, Spangle perched on the roof, hunched and lonely and missing his kind.

And out in the cold winter gardens all the worms and springtails, millipedes and nematodes and other earth-dwelling creatures moved slowly, slowly, deeper down below the frosted ground.

20
Lesson learnt

*Dormer asks for help –
but is Mistle really the right
person to advise?*

It was true that Dormer liked to spend time outdoors every day now, but that wasn't the main reason for going for a walk. Whatever anyone said, it was just too hard to see Moss suffering without trying to help.

'Who knows about despair?' thought Dormer – and that's when Mistle came to mind. After all, Mistle had endured unimaginable loss when the yew was burnt down by other Hidden Folk, and had somehow found a way to go on. The idea of turning up at the school felt scary, given that Mistle didn't smile much and had made a point of not inviting any of them over, but if there was a chance it might help, it was worth it.

Dormer slipped under the side gate and past the bins out on to the street, trying not to think about cats or Mortals or roaring death-chariots, or any of the other dangers that lay between Ash Row and the school. Luckily, the street was quiet, and by scuttling along by the kerb, with several pauses to look around, Dormer made it safely to the top of Ash Row, slipped through the school fence to the playground, and crouched behind a discarded crisp packet.

Last time the Hidden Folk had been at the school it had been pitch black and deserted, but now there were Mortal children of different ages gathered in groups, some playing on the climbing frames and some sitting on a group of benches, talking and laughing. They wore a uniform under their winter coats, and most had woolly hats and gloves. Dormer looked carefully for Ro, Ben or even Maya, but didn't recognize any of them at all.

'For whom do you seek?' came a sudden warble from behind Dormer, who jumped approximately three centimetres in the air. A blackbird a lot like Mr B had appeared on the tarmac, his bright, yellow-rimmed eyes fixed inquisitively on Dormer's face.

'Oh . . . hello. You gave me a fright!'

'A thousand apologies. I wished merely to offer you assistance. Am I to take it that you desire an audience with that one who is of your own kind, namely Mistle?'

'Erm . . . yes, that's right. How did you know?'

'An astute guess, no more,' said the blackbird. 'What, may I ask, is your name?'

'I'm Dormer – nice to meet you.'

'Likewise, indeed. You may call me Professor Merula.' Here the blackbird gave an elaborate bow, then drew himself up tall. 'Having been born and raised in an educational establishment, I consider myself something of a sage, something of a mentor, something of a—'

'Hang on, aren't you – oh, what was it? That's it! Aren't you *Turdus*?'

Immediately the bird deflated, and even his voice seemed to change.

'Yeah, all right, that's me.'

Dormer grinned. 'Mistle told us about you. You add a special twizzle to your songs that the children like, don't you?'

'That's right. I can't do it now, though – it's winter. I won't be singing until spring.'

'Fair enough. But – don't you like your name?'

'Oh, I shouldn't complain,' sighed the blackbird. 'It's just . . . it isn't very dignified, and I want to be a very dignified sort of creature. I try to set a good example to the children, you know?'

Just then a bell rang and the children began going back inside.

'Anyway,' said Dormer, 'would you mind showing me where Mistle lives? Or you could pass on the message that I'm here, if you think it would be better. I know not everyone likes unexpected visitors, and I haven't been invited.'

'Are you a friend or a foe?'

'Friend!' said Dormer quickly. 'I live in one of the gardens on Ash Row, with Moss, Burnet and Sorrel. Mistle's been advising us on something for a few weeks now, but it's all gone wrong and I – I need some help.'

'Hmm, that sounds serious,' said Turdus. 'Come this way – and let's hurry, before the next set of children come out.'

They crossed the playground to a wall near the main entrance, where a black plastic pipe led down from the gutters that ran along the edge of the roof.

'Up you go,' said Turdus. 'There's a way in at the top. I'll meet you there.'

As the blackbird flew up to the guttering, Dormer began to scale the downpipe. Behind it, little pegs – matches or nails – had been wedged into the brickwork to create a useful sort of ladder.

It didn't take Dormer long to get to the top.

'In there,' said Turdus, gesturing with his yellow beak to a dark gap behind the soffit. 'Don't be afraid.'

'I'm not,' said Dormer. 'I'm used to Mortal buildings!' And in they went.

A narrow passageway ran along the inner edge of the roof, under the tiles, and the two of them crept along it, the blackbird's claws making a scratchy sound. It made Dormer think of the badger sett, and being found by Burnet in the darkness, and how a firm friendship had taken root once they'd admitted what they were really worried about. Perhaps one day Mistle would do the same.

'Through there,' chirped Turdus. And there in front of Dormer, in the gap between some ceiling tiles and the roof timbers above, was a vast, low space. A few of the tiles had been shifted very slightly so that shafts of light filtered up from the classroom below – as well as the sound of Mortal voices, both that of a grown-up and of various children, too.

In the middle of the space a black-clad figure was lying on its front, facing away from them, as if dead.

'*Shhhhh!*' Mistle said, waving one arm at them without looking over. Turdus and Dormer stopped.

'You mustn't mind,' whispered Turdus. 'It's always like this when the children are learning something interesting. Mistle's been listening in for so many cuckoo summers now.'

'But how? They're speaking Mortal language,' whispered Dormer.

'Yes, but if you peek down, you can see the big Mortal draw things on the wall thingy, and sometimes there are moving pictures and all sorts. If you keep at it long enough, you can sort of get the drift. Well, Mistle claims to be able to, anyway; I've never really bothered with it, despite being brought up here.'

'You grew up here?' said Dormer, looking around at the bare ceiling cavity stretching out around them. 'It doesn't seem like the sort of place a blackbird would raise its young.'

'Oh, it isn't. Apparently, when I was an egg, I was in a nest in one of the playground trees. But not long after I hatched, I must have fallen out. Mistle found me on the tarmac, close to death in the hot sunshine, and carried me all the way up here – *and* it was playtime! – and then raised me single-handedly.'

'Wow! So Mistle's your foster-parent!' said Dormer.

'That's right,' chirped Turdus, proudly.

Just then Mistle got up, and greeted them both with a nod.

'Turdus. Dormer.'

'Hello, Mistle,' replied Dormer. 'What a lovely home you have. So – so open-plan and, er, minimalistic. Anyway, sorry for barging in.'

'What can I do you for?'

'I . . . I was hoping for some advice.'

Without saying a word, Mistle turned and walked away. Moss looked at Turdus for guidance.

'Well, go on, follow!' said the blackbird. 'I'll see you later.' And off he hopped, back the way they'd come.

Dormer tiptoed across the classroom ceiling to the far corner. And there, tucked behind a wooden beam, was Mistle's real home: a cosy little room jam-packed with the most interesting things Dormer had ever seen. There were pencil rubbers in the shape of robots and foxes and lemons, sweets still in their wrappers, hair scrunchies, plastic dinosaurs, pencils, pen lids, a cherry lip balm, Blu-Tack, paperclips of all shapes and sizes, a single wireless earbud, some old-fashioned ink cartridges stacked on their sides like dusty wine bottles, and, hanging on the wall like a picture, a badge that read 'I ♥ WOMBLES'.

'Wow, this is amazing! No wonder you don't want to move in with us,' said Dormer. 'What is all this stuff?'

'Absolutely no idea, for the most part,' said Mistle. 'I'm still trying to work it out. Perhaps Sorrel can come and help me one day. Anyway, sit down.'

Against one wall was a sofa made of a fluffy pencil case; as they both took a seat, the marbles inside it shifted and clacked.

Now that the time had come to explain, Dormer suddenly felt tearful, and found it almost impossible to begin.

'Take your time,' said Mistle, in a voice that almost sounded kind.

'It's Moss. And Burnet, too, of course. Oh, Mistle, I think – I think they've given up, and I'm just so worried about them! I don't know what to do – and I – I thought of you, because . . .'

'Of course they've given up. And about time too.'

'What?!'

'I knew there wasn't a yew tree anywhere near here. Don't you think I'd have known about it, if there was? Burnet may have roped in Spangle to help, but I've got Turdus, and he's flown over the entire neighbourhood checking, just in case. It was a wild goose chase from the start.'

'A – what?'

'Never mind. As for Moss – well, Pan bless anyone who tries that hard, but saving the Wild World by making one garden better was never going to work.'

'But – but it's worth doing, surely? Every wildflower seed, every chrysalis, every baby vole matters . . .'

'Of course all voles matter. Nobody's saying they don't, and the same for the bees and everything else. But it would take too long, and there isn't enough time.'

'What do you mean?'

'The Wild World is emptying out – and that includes us.'

'But – but the fading – you started to come back, and so did Burnet . . .'

Mistle shrugged. 'I don't understand it either. Some kind of weird quirk, that's all. It doesn't change anything. I'm sorry, Dormer, but sometimes the kindest thing to do is tell someone the truth.'

Dormer sat for a while, head in hands, trying to take it in.

'Why did you help with our plan, then, if you knew it was pointless?'

A catch came into Mistle's voice. 'I – I was lonely. All this time I lived here, I thought the three of them in the garden didn't want to know me – and then there you all were, being friendly – well, apart from the attack bats. I wanted to spend time with some of my own kind, that's all.'

There was a long silence.

'I – I came here to ask you to help cheer Moss and Burnet up,' said Dormer, slowly and haltingly. 'I love Moss, you see, and I thought you'd be able to tell me how you overcame despair, how you learnt to carry on.'

'This *is* how you carry on,' said Mistle, bluntly. 'You just . . . live with it, and wait.'

'Wait for what?'

But Mistle wouldn't say.

21
Whiteout

Ash Row is transformed,
and a dear friend departs.

The snow began to fall at around midnight, sifting down from a night sky thick with heavy clouds that blanketed the constellations: the sturdy Plough, the small bright cluster of Cassiopeia, the figure the Wild World knew as Pan – all were lost behind a heavy press of snow clouds. At first it was as fine as icing sugar, but soon the flakes got larger and began to clump together as they fell, swirling under Ash Row's streetlights and dancing in the headlights of the few cars that were out that late.

Because the ground was truly cold, the snow settled, building up slowly between the blades of grass until the lawns in the back gardens were white and even, icing the roofs and bonnets of the parked cars, and painting a thick white rime on the bare black branches of the trees. The snow formed rounded hummocks on the fence posts and wheelie bins, and put lids on all the leafy shrubs; it muffled sound, and, in just a few hours of darkness, it totally transformed the world.

Moss woke up when the very first hint of a weak winter sun appeared on the horizon in the east, for dozing so much in the daytime made it hard to sleep much at night. Immediately something felt different, though it was hard to say what: perhaps it was the quality of the light filtering in through the skylight in the main chamber, which seemed whiter than usual, somehow, or perhaps it was the total lack of sound.

Feeling more alert and curious than at any time in the last week, Moss crept into the main chamber and looked up. Something seemed to be covering the skylight, something dense and white, but which still let light through. There was an interesting new smell, too, something clean and fresh and wet. What on Pan's great earth could it be?

Without waking any of the others, Moss decided to have a quick look - just to be reassured that everything was normal, and it was safe to go back to bed. But, on flinging open the door at the top of the steps, Moss gasped in utter surprise and delight: not only was everything white and cold, it was breathtakingly perfect and beautiful, as though everything that had gone wrong could somehow be forgotten. The complicated, difficult everyday world was hidden, for a while at least, from sight.

Moss was gazing at Ro's garden, mouth open, taking it all in, when a voice breathed, 'Wow.' It was Dormer, who'd been woken by the cold draught from the open door, and had come up the steps to investigate.

'I know right,' said Moss.

Dormer pulled the door shut behind them, and took Moss's hand.

'What *is* it?' asked Moss. 'I mean, I can feel that it's natural and good, but – have you ever seen this before?'

'It's happened a few times since I gave up sleeping through the winter. It's called snow.'

'Where does it come from?'

'It falls from the sky, like rain.'

'No way!' said Moss, gazing up at the grey sky, which now had a faint smudge of lemon in the east.

'I know.' Dormer grinned. 'It doesn't seem likely somehow, does it?'

'And does it stay like this all winter?'

'Oh no – it might only last for a few days, or even just a morning. Depends what the weather does. Burnet'll have a better idea how long it might be before it melts.'

'That's a thought – we should go and wake the others,' said Moss. 'I wonder if they've ever seen anything like this before!'

'Wait,' said Dormer, grasping Moss's arm. 'Let's let them sleep on for a bit. Don't you want to play?'

Moss gazed out at the white garden. A cold and wintry sun was rising, its weak rays making the blanket of snow sparkle. Was it right to have fun when everything felt so sad – was it even possible? But, on the other hand, how cool would it be to leave the first set of footprints! And what if the—

Just then, a large wet snowball hit Moss squarely on the ear. Dormer shrieked with laughter and ran towards the wildflower patch. Without even stopping to think, Moss scooped up a big handful of snow, squeezed it together, and followed, yelling.

For the next ten minutes, as they pushed snow down each other's backs, dived head-first into pillowy drifts and slid down icy inclines, all the two friends felt was joy.

'Oh yes, I've seen it before, but only when it's come especially early or especially late,' said Burnet.

'Me too,' said Sorrel. 'You should see the Folly in the snow! It's so beautiful. It tinkles along between humped, snowy banks, and one time the edges froze and turned to ice, and part of the Oak Pool, too. It was amazing.'

The four Hidden Folk were sitting on the very top of the snowy log pile in which so many of the smaller Garden People were hibernating. The sun was up, but the lights hadn't yet come on in Ro's house, or in Ben and Maya's next door. Burnet and Sorrel had joined in with Moss and Dormer's game for a bit, and now they'd all run off some of their excitement, they'd decided to have a rest.

'The *best* thing about snow is all the animal prints,' said Burnet, who seemed, like Moss, to have been re-energized by the snow. 'It's amazing! You can see what everyone's been up to – where the birds have hopped, where the foxes have walked, where the mice have run. Once I found a set of wood-pigeon prints, and then the marks in the snow left by its wings as it took off!'

'Woah,' said Moss.

'Speaking of birds . . .' said Dormer, as Spangle landed on a twig sticking out of the log pile and folded his wings up tidily.

'All right, Bosses, what's occurring?' he cheeped.

'Snow, mostly,' said Moss. 'It's amazing!'

'Oh yeah, I forgot you might not've seen it. Fun for playing in, I'm sure, but it don't half make it hard for a bird to catch a meal.'

'We've got some smoked grasshopper legs, haven't we, Moss? Shall I fetch you one?' asked Dormer.

'Wouldn't say no.'

'How are you getting on, old friend?' asked Moss, when Dormer had returned with Spangle's snack. 'We haven't seen much of you in the last few days.'

'Oh, y'know,' said the starling, shrugging and looking away.

'Are you still disappointed that we didn't find a yew tree?' asked Burnet, sympathetically. 'I completely understand.'

'Nah. I mean, it's a shame for you lot, obviously. But it ain't that. I'm . . . well, sounds stupid. But I've been feeling lonely. I know I've got you lot, but

I've been missing other starlings. My people, innit? My gang, my tribe.'

The four Hidden Folk crowded around the sad little bird, comforting him with hugs and strokes and kind words until he flapped his wings impatiently and hopped out of their reach.

'All right, all right, hands off my flight feathers! Sheesh.'

'It's not too late for you to make for the coast if you want to,' said Burnet. 'I'd say the weather's set fine and cold for the next few days – good flying conditions.'

'Cheers, Boss, but it's too late. All the birds from across the seas will have got there already. They'll have made friends by now – I won't fit in. Especially arriving alone, you get me?'

'Alone, you say?' asked Moss, who was peering at the sky in the west.

'Yeah, bit weird turning up to things late and on your tod, I find.'

Burnet stood up and looked westwards too, one hand up to shield out the low winter light. 'Um, Spangle . . .'

'Anyway, I hate to sit around moping, so I came to find you lot, see what you fancied doing.'

'*Spangle!*' said Sorrel and Dormer, together,

standing up on the logs and looking past him.

'WHAT?' yelled the little bird, as, with a breath-taking rush of wings, a babble of voices and a splatter of bird poos, a hundred, two hundred star-lings – more! – rushed out of the sky and settled all around them in the sheltering trees and berry-laden bushes of the garden. They were black against the white snow and their weight bent the twigs and branches down; they squabbled and pecked at one another good-humouredly, and then, within just a few seconds, they settled . . . and were quiet.

Spangle simply stared with his beak open, while the four Hidden Folk gazed at them all, grinning. Sorrel and Moss's hands had flown up to cover their mouths, and Burnet was jumping up and down.

'A murmuration! A murmuration!' Dormer whispered, over and over.

'What's that?' came a voice from the flock, as a very beautiful and very old female bird hopped down from a twig and approached the log pile.

'The sky ballet,' said Dormer. 'Sorry – pleased to meet you, I'm Dormer. And this is—'

'Oh, we know who you all are,' she said. 'Sky ballet, is it? I'm sure something can be arranged.'

Spangle still hadn't said anything, and Moss gave him a nudge. In the presence of so many new faces, the usually confident bird was feeling terribly shy.

'All right,' he managed.

The other starling laughed, a fast series of amused beeps and clicks. 'Hello, Spangle,' she said. 'I don't think we've met, have we? I'm Lustre, and I have nine cuckoo summers behind me. I lead this flock, and we've been sent to take you east.'

'Sent? Who by?'

'Never mind that. Are you coming?'

'But—'

'They'll be all right, I promise.'

'How—'

'Trust me,' she said, with a smile in her voice.

Spangle looked at the four Hidden Folk, who were all holding hands.

'I can't go,' he whispered.

'Yes, you can,' said Burnet, reassuringly, and Moss nodded, smiling through tears.

'I can't!' Spangle repeated. 'We haven't found the right trees yet, and your old garden's done for, and you lot might not – you might not . . .'

The little bird pushed his beak into his chest feathers and sobbed.

Moss threw both arms around him, hugging him and kissing the small, soft feathers of his cheek.

'Don't worry, Spangle – Lustre is right, we'll be fine. You need to go and be with your friends now. We'll still be here when you come back in spring, just you wait and see.'

'We will, honest,' added Dormer.

'Promise,' said Sorrel.

'You *can't* promise, though, can you?' said Spangle, sniffing and hiccupping a bit from crying. 'That's the thing.'

Sorrel and Burnet looked at one another. They were still only partly visible: Burnet's legs had not come back, and Sorrel was still missing both left limbs.

'We'll do our absolute best to be here,' said Burnet. 'I can promise that.'

'I'm about to invent something, anyway,' said Sorrel. 'A – a re-visibility machine! It'll be amazing. I've already worked out exactly how to do it, I just . . . I hadn't got round to telling anyone yet.'

It wasn't true, and all of them knew it. But they also knew that Spangle would only get lonelier as the weeks went by. It was long past time for him to be a starling again, and do what starlings do in winter: flock together, roost together, swap stories and news, and at last moult into a smart new set of petrol-coloured feathers, ready for spring.

'It's time, Spangle,' said Lustre, kindly. 'Are you ready to fly with us?'

One by one, the Hidden Folk stepped forward and hugged Spangle, all of them trying not to cry.

'Keep safe,' said Moss. 'We'll miss you.'

'See you in spring,' said Burnet, before choking up and turning away.

'See you in spring!' they all cried, as the whole flock, with Spangle in their midst, jumped into the air in a roar of beating wings, and funnelled up into the winter sky above the garden, wheeling further and further, high over Ash Row.

And then something magical happened. As the flock became a distant cloud against the white sky, it began to change shape, all the tiny black dots that were individual birds coming together to form one dark mass. It flew apart into a net, then collapsed into a bubble; it stretched to make an oval, became tall and thin for a moment, then pulsed outwards into an almost sphere. It was a sky ballet, and it was amazing. Watching it, Moss's heart expanded and soared, filled with love for the little starling who was at last with his own people, part of the flock he had so longed for, making beautiful, fleeting, unforgettable shapes in the winter sky.

22
Rowan

In which everyone comes out to play.

The starling murmuration was over, and the flock long gone, by the time any of the children of Ash Row had woken up and looked out of their windows. But as the Mortal day began, out they came into their gardens, some slowly and cautiously, some yelling with excitement, some peering carefully and curiously at the tell-tale footprints and clues left by usually secretive creatures in the blanket of white. Some children rushed out without their gloves or woolly hats, and were called back in and told off; at least one pair of fluffy animal slippers got soggy and were ruined. But, as everyone knows, snow is one of the very best things in the Wild World and it must be enjoyed to the absolute maximum, because who knows how long it'll last, or when it will come back?

Burnet and Sorrel were sitting on a log watching Moss and Dormer make a snowbird. They had tried to give it a tail like Spangle's, but, although short compared to a wagtail's or even a blackbird's, it was still a bit ambitious and had made the back end of the sculpture collapse. When Ro came out of her house, Dormer blew on the white flute to signal to her where they were. She scooped up a handful of snow and ran to the end of the garden, leaving huge Mortal footprints behind her.

'*Snooooow!*' she shouted, and threw a snowball squarely at a tree trunk, where it exploded with a puff of white. As they all cheered, she crouched down next to them and grinned.

'Isn't it brilliant!' she began. 'Dad says it's a snow day and I don't have to go to school, which is basically amazing, because there's no way I was going to miss the snow anyway. It's only my second ever time of properly seeing it, though Dad says it happened once when I was a baby. What are you playing?'

'We're making a snowbird,' said Moss, 'but it's gone a bit wrong.'

'It's more of a snowlump, isn't it?' said Dormer, standing back and looking at it critically. 'Oh well.'

Ro put her head on one side and looked closely at

207

them. 'Are you all right?' she asked. 'You seem sad.'

'Oh – we're all right,' said Burnet, smiling bravely. 'A friend of ours has gone on a trip, that's all. We're going to miss him.'

'Is he coming back?'

'In spring.'

'Well, that's all right, then. Hey, did you know Ben and Maya are moving out tomorrow?'

'Tomorrow!' said Burnet, and Moss added, 'So soon?'

'All their toys are in boxes and they're only allowed to have one each until they unpack in their new house. Ben's got his bunny and Maya's got a fox you can put in the microwave and cuddle in bed.'

One of the things the Hidden Folk had found interesting and surprising about the children they had got to know was their habit of playing with pretend wild creatures, even if they didn't show much interest in them in real life. They were getting used to it now, though none of them had the faintest idea what a microwave was. Some Mortal things were just too hard to understand.

'Ben really loves that bunny,' said Burnet now. 'I would have liked to have taken him to meet a real rabbit. They're excellent company, but you can't carry them around by one ear.'

'Shall I go round and see if he wants to come and play?' asked Ro.

'Wait,' said Dormer. 'If it's their last day, let's go and play in their garden. They'll need to say good-bye to it.'

'All right, folks,' said Ro, standing up. 'Meet you round there. OK?'

Ben and Maya's mum and dad were taking them tobogganing after lunch, but the three children had a brilliant morning building a snowman by rolling two balls of snow around the lawn, leaving wiggly lines of exposed green grass. Moss, Burnet, Sorrel and Dormer helped by looking for nice round stones for the snowman's eyes, and finding a good stick for its nose. They brought their finds to Ben or Ro, as Maya was still completely oblivious to them; she didn't seem to notice Mr and Mrs B hopping around and picking up insects from the newly exposed lawn, either. Even when she caught Ben talking to Moss, she just joked to Ro about her little brother and his 'imaginary friends'. But the others just looked at one another and smiled.

When the snowman was finished, the four Hidden Folk went to sit under the evergreen shrub, while Maya took off her purple scarf and wrapped it around his neck.

'Don't forget to get it back before you leave tomorrow!' said Ro, in Mortal language.

'I think I'm going to leave it here,' said Maya. 'It can be an offering – like the ones the Romans did. Or just something to prove to whoever comes next that I lived here once.'

'Are you sad to be going?' Ro asked.

'*I* am,' said Ben. 'I'm really sad.'

'Yeah,' said Maya. 'I didn't think I would be, but I am. Our new house is really nice, and my room is loads bigger, but there's nowhere in the garden for my trampoline.'

'At least you're not changing schools,' said Ro. 'That's the main thing.'

The two girls smiled at one another. Things had changed over the last few weeks, and although they didn't know each other really well yet, there was the start of a friendship. As it turned out, they'd be friends all the way through school, and even when they were grown-ups – but neither of them knew that yet.

'Maya, did you know that there were two nests in

our garden this spring?' said Ben.

His sister shook her head.

'They're empty now, but there was a wren's nest and a dunnock's nest,' Ben continued, proudly. 'Will there be nests in our new garden?'

'I don't know,' replied Maya. 'But—'

'And did you know there's a family of house mice and they had seven babies?'

'No. But, Ben, how did you—'

'And there are little paths made by voles? Oh! Maybe we can see their footprints now it's snowy. Let's go and look! Come on, Maya, I'll show you!'

Of course, the four Hidden Folk hadn't understood a word of this conversation, but as the little boy led his sister around the garden, peering at bird prints and cats' paw marks and the little scurrying trails made by rodents, they understood exactly what he was doing: he was introducing her to the secret world of the Garden People, a world he'd only recently begun to see himself.

'Yay!' said Ro, smiling happily at the four of them. 'Maya likes nature! Look!'

'It's the snow – it makes everything seem more interesting,' said Moss, nodding knowledgeably. 'Plus, it makes you feel really nice inside.'

'It's just a shame they're leaving tomorrow,' said

Burnet, sadly. 'She won't have a chance to get to know all the Garden People, and soon it'll be too late.'

'It's still a really good thing,' said Sorrel. 'Who knows who they might meet in their new garden? I like the thought of them both looking out for the creatures that live there.'

Just then the back door opened and Ben and Maya's mum called them in for lunch. 'Would you like to eat with us too, Rowan?' she asked. 'There's plenty.'

'I'll just go and ask my dad,' said Ro, and ran next door.

Ben and Maya ran towards the house. But at the back door, Maya happened to glance back to where the Hidden Folk sat, cross-legged, under the evergreen shrub. And suddenly – for the first time – she seemed to be looking directly at them, her face alight with wonder and surprise.

'Ben! Ben!' she said, tugging at her little brother's sleeve, but he ignored her: he was too busy trying to get out of his wellies, one of which had got stuck.

'I didn't even know Ro was really called Rowan,' Ben said, kicking one leg up and down and not listening to his sister.

Moss stood up and raised a tentative hand, to wave.

'In you both come,' said their mum. 'What are you staring at, Me-me?'

'Oh – nothing,' said Maya. 'I just . . . I thought I saw something, that's all.'

23
Yew

*Things don't always end the
way you expect them to . . .*

That afternoon, Rowan and her dad, and Maya and Ben and their parents, all went to the park, where there was a snowy slope to slide down. Maya and Ben shared a wooden toboggan, bought for them years ago by their grandma and grandpa; it was only the second time it had been used, and it was great fun. Rowan had a plastic tray, which, it turned out, slid down the slippery hill far faster than the toboggan, and you could also spin around on it if you were brave enough. So they swapped and took turns, and played with the other children too, some of whom had orange plastic sleds, or even bodyboards; one or two were having great fun sliding down on just bin bags.

When they got home, the children all had hot baths, and before long it was time for dinner. But just before sitting down to eat with her dad, Ro managed to slip out into the garden for a moment. The snow hadn't melted yet, and it glimmered palely in the light of the moon and stars. All around her, birds were roosting, their feathers fluffed up against the cold: three dunnocks in the thick ivy that grew up one fence, a pair of robins in one of Ro's woven roosting pockets tucked into a shrub, and a wood pigeon in a tree overhead. The entire sparrow clan were packed into three of the bird boxes for warmth, all higgledy-piggledy, while in another, eleven tiny wrens were trying to get comfy, despite stepping on each other's heads.

Shivering a bit, Ro crunched to the end of the garden in her slippers, her arms folded against the chill.

'Moss!' she whispered, in the Wild Argot. 'Dormer! Anyone there?'

There came a faint few notes from a tiny flute made from the straw of an old drinks carton, and she followed the sound. Five Hidden Folk were sitting cross-legged in a space cleared of snow next to the log pile: Moss, Burnet, Sorrel and Dormer, and Mistle, who had come to visit earlier in the afternoon and had been telling them some of the things the children had been learning at school –

215

including the fact that the world was a globe, and that duck-billed platypuses existed. The first made total sense, but the second they all found hard to believe.

In the centre of the little group was a pebble that had been heated up on a campfire and still radiated warmth. It was Burnet's idea – a clever way to stay cosy without lighting a fire after dark, when it might be seen.

'Hello, everyone,' Ro said, crouching down. 'I can't stay long. Oh, hi, are you Mistle – do you live at my school?'

'Yup,' said Mistle tersely, who had been persuaded to come over and meet a Mortal by Dormer. 'Now, what do you know about yew trees?'

'Yew trees?' Ro asked, looking confused.

'Yes – you're in the prophecy, so the others think you must know of a magic one,' continued Mistle.

'What prophecy?'

'*Rowan and yew will make it anew.* It seems you're Rowan. So where's the yew?'

'What?' said Ro, exasperated. 'Make *what* anew?'

Moss stepped in. 'We didn't know your full name was Rowan, you see – Ben only just told us. And . . .'

'Did you think it was Rowena? Everyone does, until I explain. Or Rochelle, or Róisín.'

'No, we just . . .'

'I'm named after a tree, if that helps – a magic one. There's one not far away – I can show you, if you like?'

'We found it ages ago, but it didn't make much difference,' said Burnet. 'Thanks anyway.'

'Oh. Well, I can ask my dad about yew trees, or I could look them up online. But I don't really know what you're talking about when you say "prophecy". I'm sorry.'

'What did I tell you?' said Mistle to the others.

'It just seems like too much of a coincidence for her to be called Rowan, that's all I'm saying,' said Moss, in the voice of someone who's said something umpteen times already.

'Anyway, did you have a nice afternoon?' said Dormer, to change the subject. Clearly, Ro didn't know anything, and the last thing they needed was an argument – not after all they'd been through.

'It was brilliant! We went tobogganing. Dad said we were all good at it, but really I was the best. Ben landed in a snowdrift and the snow went right up his nose and he sneezed about twenty times – it was so funny!'

Everyone laughed at that, and even Mistle smiled.

'Anyway, I just came out to say, shall we play again tomorrow, if there's no school? And if there is school, will you show me where you live, Mistle? I won't tell anyone, promise.'

'It's way over your head – you won't be able to see,' said Mistle, bluntly.

'Oh,' said Ro, a bit taken aback.

'Don't worry, Ro, none of us have seen where Mistle lives,' said Moss, comfortingly.

'Well, except me,' said Dormer.

'Yes, but you were uninvited,' said Mistle.

There was an awkward silence. Eventually, Sorrel elbowed Mistle, who relented slightly.

'All right, Ro, how about this – you know the playground blackbird?'

'The one who copies our ringtones?'

'Do you want to be introduced? He'll sit on your shoulder at playtime if I ask him to. You can be friends with him instead – he's nicer than me.'

'Oh, I'd love that! I hate the way all the birds and animals are scared of me. It would be amazing to start making friends with them, one by one by one! What's his name?'

'Turdus.'

Ro dissolved into giggles for a moment, as did Moss and Dormer.

'I'll have you know, it's the perfect name for him!' said Mistle, sternly. 'I don't know why everyone thinks it's so funny, I really don't.'

There was the sound of the back door opening, and Ro's dad called her name.

'Sorry, I have to go – it's dinner time,' she said, standing up. 'See you tomorrow! Hope you all stay cosy and warm tonight!'

The stars that made up Pan's head, shoulders, arms and belt, with pipe attached, were rising over the rooftops to the south-west. Huddled beneath Pan's gaze, at the end of the snowy garden of 51 Ash Row, the five Hidden Folk were starting to think about calling it a day.

'At least we tried to save the Wild World,' said Moss. 'We really did.'

Dormer looked over, concerned, but Moss didn't look sad. That feeling had passed, like melting snow.

'We absolutely, *totally* did our best,' agreed Burnet. 'Especially me.'

'That's all anyone can do,' said Sorrel. 'I'm proud of us. I'm proud of how we worked together, and how brave and resourceful we were. And how we kept each other safe.'

'So you should be,' said Mistle, gruffly. 'You've reminded me what it's like to have friends, and to trust people. I – I don't hate it that you're going to live here.'

'And it's not such a bad thing after all, to live as the animals do,' said Moss. 'To just enjoy our time in the Wild World, for however long we have left.'

Just then a dark shape materialized silently at the edge of their little circle, blotting out the stars. Eyes wide, they all froze – until, with a yell, Burnet recognized two triangular ears and a glimmer of white chest fur.

'Vesper! I knew you'd find us, I *knew* it!'

Moss, Dormer, Burnet and Sorrel rushed over to embrace their dear friend the vixen. Laughing, she lay down and let them climb on her and pull her whiskers; but when Mistle shyly stepped forward she just touched noses with the newcomer, as if she knew that here was someone who'd been hurt, and who needed their own space.

Then, 'How good it is to see you all at last,' came

an unfamiliar voice from the dark garden. Moss's heart thumped.

A second figure stepped forward. It was about as tall as your hand is long, and was dressed in leaves which had been waxed, burnished and overlapped cleverly, like the softest armour imaginable. Its face was both impossibly ancient and incredibly young, all at the same time.

Nobody said anything. Trembling, Moss took Dormer's hand.

'Do none of you know me?'

In the silence, the first flakes of a new snowfall began to drift down as a black bank of cloud moved over the stars.

'Perhaps you'll recognize my companion,' said the figure, stepping aside to stand with Vesper. She didn't seem at all surprised, but was watching what happened carefully.

Out of the darkness came a faint glimmer of white hair, almost lost in the drifting, starlit flakes. Atop the hair was a slightly wonky hat made from a conical pencil-shaving, and below it was a flowing green robe.

Moss dropped Dormer's hand and stepped forward, eyes blurred with sudden tears.

'Cumulus? Is that – is that really you?'

'It is,' said Cumulus, whose dear, beloved and completely visible face was streaming with happy tears. 'Oh, how I've missed you! I've missed you all *so* much.'

When at last the hugging and crying were beginning to die down, the leaf-clad figure spoke: 'My name is Robin Goodfellow. I suspect you already knew that, deep inside.'

Moss couldn't quite let go of Cumulus's hand, and was holding Dormer's, too. Burnet was holding Cumulus's other hand, and one of Sorrel's. When they all turned to face Robin and Vesper they were still a bit wobbly from the reunion. Only Mistle stood apart.

'Have you noticed anything?' Robin asked them, smiling.

'You mean, apart from Cumulus being here?' asked Moss, wiping away a tear. 'No, not really! That's all I care about right now.'

'Nothing at all? What about you, Burnet? And you, Sorrel?'

Perplexed, the two stared at each other – and that's when they realized that all their missing parts were visible again, just as Cumulus was.

'The fading! It's been reversed!' cried Burnet. 'Sorrel, look at my feet! Look at my feet, everybody!'

Sorrel held out one arm and stared at it in absolute joy, and then stuck out a foot and wiggled it, whispering, 'My left side is back! My left side is back!'

'And you, Mistle?' said Robin Goodfellow, quietly. 'Have you noticed anything?'

'No,' said Mistle, with a shake of the head.

'Are you sure?'

'My heart is still missing,' said Mistle. 'I'm not like the others, you see – I'm broken. I've been broken since I lost my tree.'

'Nobody's broken for ever,' said Robin kindly. 'Not if you don't want to be. Come here.'

Reluctantly, Mistle went over to Robin, muttering, 'I don't like hugs, by the way.'

Robin's expression was one of boundless tenderness and sympathy.

'I know.'

'Are you going to do magic on me?'

'No.'

'What, then?'

Robin gazed deep into Mistle's eyes. 'Mistle, guardian of the yew tree, you are beloved among our people, now and for ever. You may be changed, but you are not broken. Everything about you is as exactly it should be.'

Mistle tried to laugh bitterly, but was overtaken by tears. 'But I – I'm different from all the others . . . I don't want to play Acorn Hop, I don't like snowball fights, I want to live by myself!'

Robin smiled, and said it again. '*Everything about you is exactly as it should be.* You are not broken; this is just who you are, and we love you for it. Don't we?'

And when the others came forward to say they agreed, at last a fragile new warmth began to spread in Mistle's chest.

'Thank you for stopping us from fading out of the Wild World,' said Moss shyly to Robin Goodfellow. Vesper had gone off hunting, and the Hidden Folk were down in the underground house. Sorrel was proudly showing Cumulus and Mistle around while Burnet got a fire going; Dormer and Moss were preparing a celebratory meal.

'Oh, I didn't do that,' said Robin. 'You did it yourselves.'

'No, we didn't,' said Moss. 'I mean, we tried, but it all went wrong. We didn't make next-door's garden any better – that was my idea, a way of giving ourselves a new job – and although we met Rowan, we didn't find a yew tree. You know, "Rowan and yew", like in the prophecy?'

'Oh, *that*,' said Robin, eyes twinkling. 'I see what's happened. Let us feast, and then I'll explain.'

Moss laid out the meal. There was acorn bread with nut butter to start, smoked grasshopper legs, chrysalis soup (they only used empty chrysalises), honey-baked sloes with cyclamen garnish, and rose-petal pastries from the supplies Burnet had stored in the Very Big Hole. Cumulus produced a snail shell of the most delicious ivy-berry cordial, saying, 'Of course, it should really be laid down to mature for at least two cuckoo summers,' to which they all replied that sometimes a younger vintage was exactly what was needed – especially when everyone was thirsty and had missed it so much.

'So I hear you went looking for a yew tree,' said Robin to Burnet at last.

'And we failed,' said Burnet. 'I suppose Moss has told you.'

'And while you were working to fulfil the prophecy, Moss and Dormer tried to make a new role for the Hidden Folk by saving the Wild World one garden at a time, is that right?'

Moss nodded, while Dormer just said, 'Sorry,' and looked down.

'And what did you do, Sorrel?'

'I invented our house, and - and I tried to help everyone. But, as you can see, it didn't work out.'

'And yet the fading has been reversed, and Cumulus is here with you all again. Why do you think that is?'

'Perhaps Pan took pity on us,' offered Burnet.

'It wasn't that.'

'What was it, then?' asked Moss. 'Please don't say it's just a strange quirk, and we could all disappear again. I couldn't bear it - not now we've been reunited. Not now there's hope.'

'*You* did it. You have successfully created a new job for yourselves - that's why. What you're doing is really, really important, and you need to stay in the Wild World and keep doing it. Don't you understand?'

All the Hidden Folk except Cumulus looked at one another, confused.

'Eh?' said Burnet.

'Erm, what, exactly, have we been doing?' asked Moss.

'*I* haven't done anything useful, that's for sure,' said Mistle.

'Mistle,' said Robin. 'Do you remember when

226

you nearly faded away all those years ago? And then bits of you came back?'

'Yes . . .'

'You rescued a baby blackbird, you named him Turdus merula, and taught him that it was safe to be around children, and now lots of the children notice him, and they understand that he's real – as real as they are.'

'I don't understand.'

Robin turned to the others. 'There's a Mortal boy next door who can see our world now, when he couldn't before – and he's started telling his sister about it. He knows we're real too; he can *feel* we are, inside. That means he cares, and that kind of caring will change him for ever. He's on our side now, and he always will be – because of what you did.'

'Robin's right,' continued Cumulus. 'Saving the whole Wild World is too big a task for Hidden Folk – or for any wild creature, come to that. No, *our* job is to look for the kind children – the ones with enough imagination to see us, the ones who care so much that they can speak the Wild Argot, and will listen to us in turn. We can help them see that our lives matter: Hidden Folk and Garden People, Stream People and Sea People, Air People and

Underground People – *every single one of us*. That's the most important thing for Mortals to feel in their hearts – especially the young ones, because once they really know it, it will stay with them all their lives.'

'But the prophecy,' said Burnet. '*Ash, oak and thorn were at the world's dawn; rowan and yew will make it anew.* What about that?'

'You were so nearly right,' said Robin, smiling. 'It's "Rowan and *you*". *All* of you.'

'Us!' said Sorrel, laughing. 'I get it!'

'I *knew* it was about Rowan the Mortal girl!' added Moss triumphantly.

'She's important,' agreed Robin. 'She can help you find out which children at the school are kind, and safe for you to show yourselves to – because it isn't all of them, by any means, or even most. And that's not all: in twenty cuckoo summers or so, when she's grown up, she'll do more amazing things for the Wild World – just you wait and see.'

'What else can you tell us about the future?' asked Moss. 'What about our old garden – is it really going to disappear?'

'That depends,' replied Robin. 'I will say this for Mortals: they can create unexpectedly wonderful things when they put their minds to it, and quite often they do. But now, friends, it's time for me to go.'

'Go?' said Cumulus, surprised. 'I thought you were going to stay with us, and help us work out how to do this? You can't just leave, not now. We've travelled such a long way together to get here!'

'We have, old friend,' said Robin, getting up. 'But there are Hidden Folk reappearing all over the Wild World, feeling lost and confused, and I must find them and help them understand what our task is now. It will take me many cuckoo summers, and there is no time to lose.'

'But I had so many questions!' burst out Sorrel. 'About Pan, and whether there's a next place, and . . . well, everything!'

'Please stay, Robin,' said Burnet. 'How do we start? What do we do?'

'You don't need me, Burnet,' said Robin, laughing. 'Between you, you have all the skills you need. In Moss you have hope, and in Dormer, love; in Cumulus you have wisdom, and in Sorrel, skill; in Mistle you have resilience, and in you, Burnet, courage. You have a safe home, a Mortal child as your friend and helper, and a whole school of children to meet.'

'But . . . will we see you again, old friend?' asked Cumulus.

'Look for me where you least expect me,' said Robin Goodfellow. 'I am everywhere, and for ever. I believe this, and so should you.'

And with that, their guest was gone.

The Hidden Folk stayed awake late into the night, filling each other in about everything that had happened, making plans for what came next, telling jokes (mostly Burnet) and singing songs (Moss, very badly). Rarely has the Wild World witnessed a happier gathering, or one more filled with hopefulness and love. Cumulus proudly showed everyone the beginnings of a new sand grain collection, Moss kept hugging everyone, and Mistle kept smiling shyly, even trying on Cumulus's hat at one point, and reaching out to pat Burnet on the back.

At last they all began to feel tired, and Mistle decided it was time to go back to the school, to sleep. They trooped out into the snowy garden to say goodbye, and there, waiting quietly in the shadows, was Vesper, who'd come to see their friend safely home.

'Goodnight, Mistle!' 'See you tomorrow!' 'Bye, Vesper!' they all chorused quietly, and waved until the sleek fox and the little black-clad figure had slipped between the houses to the street, and out of sight.

One by one, they turned to go back in through the secret door in the log pile, until only Cumulus, Dormer and Moss were left outside in the sparkling snow.

'I've been meaning to ask you about the spring ballad, Moss,' said Cumulus. 'Have you been working on anything?'

'Of course,' replied Moss, proudly. 'It's going to describe all our adventures since leaving the Hive, including a short history of Hobs, for Dormer, explaining how we're all the part of the same family.'

'Oh! You've really done that? For me?' asked Dormer, squeezing Moss's hand.

'Well, nearly,' said Moss, holding the secret door open for the others. 'I haven't finished it yet, but it's going to be good, mainly because the word "Hob" has a lot of excellent rhymes.'

'Absolutely tremendous,' said Cumulus happily, as the door to the winter garden closed behind them. 'I can't wait to hear it. Roll on spring, eh?'

Moss and Dormer smiled at each other as they followed their old friend into the cosy dwelling. 'Absolutely,' said Moss. 'Roll on spring.'

A Note From the Author

This is a story about the secret world of wild creatures that exists all around us at every moment, something which most grown-ups (and many children) have no idea exists.

If you're a noticing kind of person, as I am, you might well pick up clues to this secret world when you're playing outside: things like neatly nibbled nutshells, interesting-looking holes and paths, mysterious droppings, or footprints in mud or snow. From these clues you can work out who you share your garden, street, playground or park with, what they've been up to, and what life is like for your smaller neighbours, whether they're feathered or furred, moist-skinned or prickly, have an armoured exoskeleton or wear an acorn-cup hat. You might even have the very great honour of giving them a helping hand one day.

But if, despite your noticingness, you find it hard to believe in Hidden Folk – perhaps because you've never seen one, and neither have any of your friends – that's completely all right. Even the brief glimpse I had was accidental, because over the course of many centuries they have perfected the art of not being observed by us. And as well as that, you might have come across some ridiculous cartoons or silly stories about magical elves and goblins, comical gnomes or flying fairies with sparkly wings, which have made you feel sure that such preposterous creatures don't exist.

And you'd be right. Hidden Folk aren't magic, and they don't have sparkly wings. They live by hunting, fishing and gathering wild foods, just as wild animals do. They have been in the Wild World since for ever, which is a lot longer than us humans, and once lived in all the different parts of these islands and in many other countries, too – although there are far fewer of them now than once upon a time.

When there were more of them and fewer of us, they were seen a little more often, and we humans gave them names, just as we named the birds and plants and insects and everything else: we called them hidden folk and little grey men, elves and fairies, goblins and gnomes, imps, sprites and, in the West Country, pixies (or piskies). The Romans referred to them as *Genii locorum*, which means 'the guardians of a place'; they were known as sidhe in Ireland, brownies in Scotland, huldufólk in Iceland and by lots of other names across Europe and beyond. But the truth is that whatever we choose to call them isn't what they call themselves.

One more thing. I'm sure it comes as no surprise to you to learn that all the birds and insects and animals and Hidden Folk can talk to one another, more or less, using what's called the 'Wild Argot': a basic language that all of nature shares. Each species speaks it slightly differently, but they can all make themselves understood by one another, and in fact the only creature that's forgotten how to communicate with the Wild World is we humans. But I suspect that, in fact, most of us have just stopped listening – which perhaps comes to the same thing.

Melissa Harrison, autumn 2021

Acknowledgements

Thank you to Barry, Rachel and everyone else at Chicken House for seeing the promise in an early sketch of this world, and helping to turn it into the two books it needed to become.

Thank you, always, to my agent Jenny Hewson, who knows what's what.

Thank you to early reader Peter Rogers, to Josie George and Isabel Chua for help with names, to Jules Howard and Su Smith for insights about otters and trains respectively, and to Nicola Guereca and Nick Redman for lending me a calm, quiet place to write when I really needed one.

I'm very grateful to the Trustees of the Estate of the late Denys Watkins-Pitchford for their kind permission to make reference to the characters from B.B.'s classic *The Little Grey Men* books – both of which I highly recommend.

Extract from *Indian Summer*, B.B. (Michael Joseph, 1984) reprinted by permission of David Higham Associates.

Watching the Wild World

SEPTEMBER

Look out for animals hiding ripe nuts and fruit so they can eat it in winter, when there isn't much food around. Squirrels and jays bury nuts and acorns; voles and mice cache seeds and hedgerow fruit in crevices like hollow tree stumps. The more berries and nuts there are, the more creatures can survive winter. Make sure not to take their stores!

OCTOBER

This is the time of the second great bird migration of the year, when billions of birds move around the globe. You might see wavering lines or arrows ('skeins') of geese high overhead, big mixed flocks of finches moving from place to place, or spot redwings, fieldfares and waxwings who have come all the way from Scandinavia to eat berries in our towns and countryside.

NOVEMBER

Where are the biggest ivy plants near you? Evergreen ivy often grows up other trees, or in hedges, using stronger plants as support for its twining stems. Mature ivies flower at this time of year, and you might find it buzzing with lots of beautiful, yellow and black striped ivy bees taking advantage of the last big nectar source of the year.

DECEMBER

Ever wondered where birds sleep (roost) at night? In winter they often huddle together for warmth, particularly small ones like wrens – sixty-one were once counted coming out of the same nest box! A clue to a roosting spot can be a small collection of white bird droppings. Above it you'll see the twig, branch or fencepost where a bird spends the night.

JANUARY

Search for bird and animal footprints in the muddy margins of puddles, or on the banks of streams (and if it snows, you can look for footprints everywhere!) Can you work out who they belong to, and what they were up to while you weren't looking? Don't forget, some might belong to dogs and cats.

FEBRUARY

Snowdrops are one of the first flowers to come out in spring, having stored all their energy over winter in a bulb underground. The tips of the green, growing shoots are tough enough to pierce frozen soil, and they contain a special chemical that acts as an antifreeze so they aren't killed by frost or snow.

More to Discover

Things to read:

The Little Grey Men by B.B.

*The Little Grey Men Go Down
    the Bright Stream* by B.B.

Animal Tracks and Signs by Preben Bang and Preben
    Dahlstrom

RSPB The Nature Tracker's Handbook by Nick Baker

Wonderland: A Year of Britain's Wildlife, Day by Day by
    Brett Westwood and Stephen Moss

How to Help a Hedgehog and Protect a Polar Bear by Jess
    French and Angela Keoghan

What to Look For in Spring by Elizabeth Jenner

What to Look For in Summer by Elizabeth Jenner

What to Look For in Autumn by Elizabeth Jenner

What to Look For in Winter by Elizabeth Jenner

An Explorer's Guide to The Lost Spells by Robert
    Macfarlane and Jackie Morris (free pdfs)
    Spring Edition: bit.ly/lost_spells_spring
    Summer Edition: bit.ly/lost_spells_summer
    Autumn Edition: bit.ly/lost_spells_autumn
    Winter Edition: bit.ly/lost_spells_winter

Things to watch:

Springwatch and *Autumnwatch* (BBC Two, ongoing)

Oak Tree: Nature's Greatest Survivor (available on
   YouTube)

Directed by Stephen de Vere:

   *Through the Garden Gate: A Diary of the English
      Countryside*

   Summer in the Meadow: Diary of a Vanishing World

   Return to the River: Diary of a Wildlife Cameraman
      (available on DVD from bit.ly/stephendevere)

Things to do:

Take part in the New Year Plant Hunt, January:
bit.ly/bray_plant

Take part in the Big Garden Birdwatch, January:
bit.ly/bray_bird

Learn to recognize the constellations:
bit.ly/bray_star

Build a bottle boat:
bit.ly/bray_boat

TRY ANOTHER GREAT BOOK FROM CHICKEN HOUSE

THE MARVELLOUS LAND OF SNERGS
by VERONICA COSSANTELI

Pip and Flora are in trouble. They have run away from the Sunny Bay Home for Superfluous and Accidentally Parentless Children – and fallen into another world altogether.

The Marvellous Land of Snergs has tree houses, cinnamon bears and wobsers – but there are also dastardly Kelps and a villain in head-to-toe purple. Their new friend is a cheerful Snerg called Gorbo. He will lead them home, if they know where home really is – and if Gorbo can remember how to get there . . .

'Warm and witty and so much FUN, it lifts the spirits. It's beautiful to look at too, making it feel a proper gift.'
NATASHA FARRANT

'. . . non-stop plot, humour, outrageous characters, jeopardy – and final satisfying happy ending.'
BOOKS FOR KEEPS

Paperback, ISBN 978-1-911490-60-9 • £6.99 ebook, ISBN 978-1-913322-66-3, £6.99

TRY ANOTHER GREAT BOOK FROM CHICKEN HOUSE

BEETLE BOY by M. G. LEONARD

Darkus can't believe his eyes when a huge insect drops out of the trouser leg of his horrible new neighbour. It's a giant beetle – and it seems to want to communicate.

But how can a boy be friends with a beetle? And what does a beetle have to do with the disappearance of his dad and the arrival of Lucretia Cutter, with her taste for creepy jewellery?

'A darkly funny Dahl-esque adventure.'
KATHERINE WOODFINE

'A wonderful book, full to the brim with very cool beetles!'
THE GUARDIAN

Paperback, ISBN 978-1-910002-70-4, £6.99 • ebook, ISBN 978-1-910002-98-8, £6.99